Marco & Rakia 2:

Not Your Ordinary Hood Kinda Love

Tina J

Copyright 2017

More Books by Tina J

A Thin Line Between Me & My Thug 1-2
I Got Luv for My Shawty 1-2
Kharis and Caleb: A Different kind of Love 1-2
Loving You is a Battle 1-3
Violet and the Connect 1-3
You Complete Me
Love Will Lead You Back
This Thing Called Love
Are We in This Together 1-3
Shawty Down to Ride For a Boss 1-3
When a Boss Falls in Love 1-3
Let Me Be The One 1-2
We Got That Forever Love
Ain't No Savage Like The One I got 1-2
A Queen & Hustla 1-2 (collab)
Thirsty for a Bad Boy 1-2
Hasaan and Serena: An Unforgettable Love 1-2
We Both End Up With Scars
Caught up Luvin a beast 1-3
A Street King & his Shawty 1-2
I Fell for the Wrong Bad Boy 1-2 (collab)
Addicted to Loving a Boss 1-3
All Eyes on the Crown 1-3
I need that Gangsta Love 1-2 (collab)
Still Luvin' a Beast 1-2
Creepin' With The Plug 1-2
I Wanna Love You 1-2
Her Man, His Savage 1-2
When She's Bad, I'm Badder 1-3
Marco & Rakia 1-2

Marco

"Rahmel, what the fuck happened out here and where's my girl?" He was standing next to me as the EMT's, put one of my guards on a stretcher.

"Man, my mom, attacked Rakia's car; Ang, beat my sister up and some dude, came outta nowhere, walked up on Rak, and made her get in the car with him."

"What the fuck, you just say?" I had him yoked up against the car.

"Marco, I know you love my cousin and trust me, if I could've saved her, I would've. I was so busy trying to get my mom and stop the fight, that none of us paid attention, to Rakia. We heard gunshots and the dude was on the ground. By the time, we looked, some guy, had her in the car, pulling off." I let him go.

"FUCK! Was she hit? Who is the dude?"

"I don't know. I've never seen him before and you know, I know everyone." I nodded because he really did.

4

Rahmel, isn't a street nigga but he was cool, with all the hood dudes. On a few occasions, I let him parlay in VIP with us, when we went out, just because he was Rakia's cousin and the only one, besides his grandmother, who looked out for her.

"What kind of car was it?"

"It was black, with tinted windows and dark enough, where I couldn't see in." I looked at Tech, who was stressing the fuck out over the shit, Cara told Ang. I had to make him stay with me and not get Ang from the station, right away. I told him, she needed time to figure shit out and he could explain it later. When a woman is that angry, its best to give her space.

"Where's your mother?"

"Man, I don't know. The bitch went running to some car and left." I nodded.

"Marco." I turned around and saw Rak's grandmother coming in my direction.

"I'm so sorry. I didn't mean for this to happen."

"What exactly happened?" She explained, how she called Rak over because she wanted the three of them to make

5

up. She was over the fighting and pettiness, between them. I understood why but I also told her, it wasn't a good idea, without having me there to protect her. Not that, I'm a savior but I damn sure am, Rakia's. She agreed and begged me to find her.

"I am. Go in the house and I'll call you, when I have her." I kissed her cheek. Tech and I, headed over to my truck and got inside.

"Who you think could have her?"

"Man, I have no idea. Rakia, doesn't have any enemies and forgave everybody, no matter how fucked up they were to her. She had to know this person or even feel like, he wasn't a threat. At least, it's what I'm thinking but the questions is; who?

We drove to the police station to get Ang and it looked like the shit was deserted. He opened the door and we walked to the captain's office. He wasn't there, which is weird because Tech called and mentioned Ang, would be coming and he said, he'd be there. The only person here right now was the old ass lady, doing dispatch. She had to be related to someone, in order

6

to have this position. We both approached her at the desk and she rolled her eyes, as if we did something to her.

"If you want something, open your mouth." Tech and I, both started laughing. How her old ass in here, talking shit?

"Yo, where the captain at?" She turned around and looked behind her and then under the desk.

"Well, he ain't in here, now is he?"

"Bitch, I'll fuck you up in here." Tech, had her by the shirt.

"Yo, let her old ass go." She had a petrified look on her face.

"Bet yo ass, ain't tough now."

"I could have you arrested?" She was shaking.

"By who? Ain't a motherfucker, in this place. What the hell is going on and where is the captain?"

"Since, you asked nicely, I guess, I could tell you." I had about enough of her ass.

"Someone shot up a police car and all available units are in route there."

"Oh word? Somebody bold as hell for that?" Just as this shit was happening, a text message came to my phone. I opened it and wasn't prepared for the shit, I saw.

"I'm gonna kill Rakia." I was ready to go. I told him to get the information needed, so we could get Ang because murder was all over my brain.

"Where's the woman who's supposed to be dropped off?" Tech asked and she gave him a sympathetic stare. I looked at him and his demeanor was unreadable.

"What?"

"The cop car, that was shot up, had a woman passenger in the back. I'm sorry." It was like all the blood drained from his face and he fell against the wall. I asked for the address, where the shooting was. I would deal with Rakia later because his news, is worse. We drove to the scene and shit was taped off. Caution tape, cops and detectives were everywhere and the coroners truck was there.

"You ok?" I asked and turned to look at him. I saw a few tears coming down his face.

"Bro, I can't get out."

8

"Tech, you have to." He sat there for a few minutes and finally opened the door.

When we made our way through the crowd, the scene was much worse, than I could imagine. Tech, stood there frozen and out the corner of my eye, I noticed someone, who in my opinion could only be there, if they were responsible. Tech, must've seen the same person, because he took off running and outta nowhere, shots rang out.

"TECHHHHHHHHHH!"

Zaire (Z)

"What's that nigga's number?" I questioned Rakia, who was balled up in a fetal position, on the couch. Hell yea, I'm the one who took her.

"I'm not giving it to you." This has been her same response for the past half hour and a nigga, was fed up. I snatched the phone out her hand, that she held onto and got his number. She didn't even have a damn lock on it.

"When did you get this?" She used to have an old ass phone, the entire time we were together. Now, she has the damn IPhone 8.

"Today. Please don't hurt him." I laughed and opened the phone book. There were only about ten numbers in it, which didn't make it hard to find his. I saved it in my phone and kept hers with me. I sent him the video of us fucking and her sucking me off. It was to hurt him and have him think, she left willingly and we were fucking at this very moment. The shit was bound to piss him off. If you're wondering why I'm coming for him, let me explain.

Exactly, three years ago to this date, my brother Dennis, was killed by Marco. See, my brother was a kingpin in Connecticut and Marco, was his plug. One day, he told me about him trying to take Marco down and become the plug himself. Of course, as his brother, I told him, he was playing with fire. Everyone in the tri state, DMV and other surrounding areas, knew exactly who he was. He wasn't a nigga, you went against and his team was one to be reckoned with.

Unfortunately, my brother, thought differently and came up with a team willing to take him down. Dennis had some of the thoroughest dudes, in our state. Some of these dudes, had so many murders under their belt, it was a miracle they were even outta jail. They swore, no one would be able to survive, after they finished. I still wasn't sure it would work out the way, Dennis planned.

The day of the so-called takedown, we all drove out to Jersey, the day before because we were going in that night. We wanted to catch the niggas off guard. The guys stayed in their

11

rooms resting up for the night, while my brother and I, stayed in ours discussing escape routes and so forth. The warehouse we planned on hitting, was supposed to receive a shipment tonight. Marco and his team, were always there to make sure, shit was running smooth. This is the information our cousin, gave us. She supposedly didn't care for Marco because he didn't like her, or some shit.

Anyway, the night it all went down was a nightmare. I tried to talk my brother out of it, but he refused to listen. I really wish, I tried harder but when your mind is set on doing something, nothing no one else says, will matter. My mother, blamed me for not making him stay back but I had to let her know too. Shit, ain't always as easy as, the way people make it seem.

"Dennis, I'm not feeling this. Something isn't right." I told him and he sucked his teeth.

"Z, I know you don't live this lifestyle, so if you wanna leave, go ahead." I was a straight A student, and on my way to one of the most prestigious schools in the country, which was Harvard.

I didn't know Marco, like that because growing up, I stayed with my father out in Connecticut. I never came to visit, due to my mother and I, not getting along. She was how would you say it? A ho! My mom, cheated on my father, while she was pregnant with me, so he says. Come to find out, she left him and came to Jersey, to be with the guy; hence the reason, Dennis and Marco met, and became best friends. My father wouldn't allow me to go with her and being my brother was a few years older than me, it's the only reason he let her take him.

Over the years, I ended up resenting her because as my mother, regardless of how her and my father worked out, she should've never left. I understand, she fell for someone else but the man, whoever he was, never should have even allowed her, to be away from her other son. What type of man would ask her to do that? My dad said, you couldn't tell my mom shit back then and let her go. Evidently, the guy cheated on my mom and moved with another woman. She brought her ass right back to Connecticut after Dennis graduated and my pops, still doesn't fuck with her. I guess, karma is a bitch.

13

"I'm not gonna leave you here."

"Then be quiet and make sure you bust your guns, when its time."

"Dennis, there's no one here. Don't you think, its odd? The guy gave you a specific time and it's a half hour passed and still, nothing. Maybe we should pull back and.-"

"Shut the fuck up, Z." He shouted in a loud whisper and pointed to the spot. A SUV truck pulled up and a few guys, got out smoking and laughing. I still wasn't feeling this. No one comes late to a drop off and if Marco, is this dude who makes no mistakes, I don't see him making one, the same night, he's supposed to get hit.

We watched the men walk in the building and later, a huge truck pulled up. The driver backed in and stepped out. You heard the back door being lifted and all of a sudden, you could hear shots being fired. However, the people dropping weren't from Marco's squad. All of Dennis team members were hitting the ground. He told me to stay put and ran off somewhere. I stayed like he said and continued listening to gunshots.

14

After it stopped, two guys walked out the shadows and stood over a guy, who I realized was my brother. I stood up to run after him, when I heard a gun cock on the back of my head. The guy told me not to move and experience from the front line, as his boss took my brother's life. I could hear Dennis begging but the dude, said no words and took his life. I felt a tear fall from my eyes. The other guy looked up and nodded. I heard the gun cock and instead of letting him kill me, I pulled my weapon out and shot him.

"You should've checked me for a weapon first." I said as he laid there, drowning in his own blood.

I ran off and to the car we drove. I sped all the way back to Connecticut and told my mom what happened. She wanted to contact the police but we both knew, if she did, we'd be dead before daylight. We both cried and waited for the cops to come. They never showed up, until a week later, stating they found him dead in a parking lot. My mom was even more hysterical after hearing they made it look like a set up. The funeral was sad and I vowed to Dennis, I would get revenge on his killer.

Needless to say, I drove to Jersey about a year ago and showed up at the club, Marco and his partner, Tech would be at. It was weird to see Rakia, there with him. I noticed how she danced with him and was about to leave and became pissed. She and I, were talking and kissed once, so why was she with this nigga? I had one of my boys shoot up inside the club and waited for people to run out, to make my way in. I wanted to look the nigga in his face, to make sure when I clapped back, it would be the right person. Little did I know, he'd knock my ass out but it's all good because now, I have his bitch, or should I say, my bitch, in my cousins' house. I sent him a nice little video about five minutes ago and I bet, he isn't happy at all.

"Why did you leave campus Rakia? You said, you were staying for the summer." She gave me a dirty look.

"Why didn't you tell me about the STD's and pubic lice you had? Why did you force me to suck your dick? Why did you cheat on me? Why did you almost hit me?" She bombarded me with questions, I couldn't answer.

I didn't know about the diseases until I got the anonymous letter. Shit, I thought, my ass was scratching from jock itch and the diseases; I had no idea who gave them to me. I had been fucking so many chicks and strapped up, only if they made me. I loved feeling the raw walls inside a woman. As far as cheating, shit, she wasn't giving up no pussy and a nigga was horny. I don't consider her sucking my dick, as forcing her. She claimed to want to be a woman in the bedroom and sucking dick is part of it. Shit, she didn't bite me or stop, so what is she talking about. As far as, almost hitting her, I wouldn't have. Yea, I yoked her up but I know my limits. Those niggas would've killed me, if I laid hands on her.

"Answer my question?" She blew her breath out.

"I needed to get away. You hurt me and space was the best thing."

"Well, you're coming back with me."

"No, Zaire. My grandmother is here and she wants me to stay."

"Man, you wanna stay in that fucked up ass environment, I pulled you from? Some lady, fucked a truck up,

17

I'm assuming is yours because she was calling you all types of bitches. The other chick, look like she hated you. And your ass was like a scared child, sitting on a curb."

"They're still my family. Can you just drop me back off? I won't tell anyone."

"Nah, you're too valuable for me."

"What?"

"I'm here for Marco and since you seem to be his new addiction; I think, you staying with me is the best thing."

"Why are you after Marco? And, I don't have anything to do with your issues." I hated when she spoke proper. She wasn't ghetto but she got on my nerves with the way she spoke.

"Just be quiet." I said and let the phone ring.

"WHO THIS?"

"Don't worry about all that. Just know, I got your girl and.-" The beep in my ear, indicated he hung up.

"This nigga hung up." She smirked.

"That's funny."

"Actually, it is."

"Why is that?"

"I guess, it shows, I'm not really his addiction after all. If I were, he would've never hung up and waited for instructions, right?" I could sense the sadness in her voice over him not taking the call serious. Don't get me wrong, Rakia is a good person; unfortunately, she got caught up with two of the wrong niggas. I noticed her wiping her eyes and roll over on the couch. Oh well. I guess we'll see what happens from here.

****

"Why is that bitch, in my house?" My cousin asked. I had fallen asleep on the chair next to her. I've been here for a couple days waiting for her to come home, to see if we were still proceeding with the plan.

"Shhhhh." I looked at the clock and it was after one in the morning.

"I'm gonna keep her, in order to get Marco."

"Z, he saw the video you sent and to my knowledge, doesn't wanna have anything else to do with her. Look." My cousin showed me a video of him standing outside what looks

19

like a crime scene, telling someone Rakia, could die for all he cared.

"So much, for her being a hostage." I said and looked at her.

"Drop her ass off and come up with a new plan." She said and walked upstairs. I stared at Rakia and shook my head. I guess, neither one of us, is good for her.

I carefully, lifted her up and placed her in my cousins' car. I didn't wanna use mine, because someone may have seen my plates. I drove over to her grandmother's house and rode down the street a few times, before pulling over to drop her off. I parked down the street, took her out the car and laid her on the ground. Anything, that happened from here on out, was on her.

I drove over to my cousins' house, switched cars and headed back to Connecticut. A new plan had to be devised and it couldn't happen here. I'd be too paranoid he'd find me, before I found him. I'm gonna make sure, my plan is airtight, unlike my brother because Marco's time, will up, soon enough.

Rakia

I woke up on the damn sidewalk and unsure, how I got here. Granted, Zaire held me hostage for a few days but why did he let me go? I thought people who kidnapped you, kept you around until they received money or something. But then again, Marco hung up on him, when he mentioned having me. I smirked because it was funny; however, when I thought about it, it wasn't because he wasn't coming to save me. Was I not worth, him saving? I thought he said, he'd protect me at all times. Whatever the case; at least I'm home.

I crept onto my grandmothers' porch and used the key under the rug, to get in. I knew, she'd be sleep because it was so late. I made me a plate of food, hoping she wouldn't hear the microwave go off and took it and a water bottle, to my room. I had no cell phone, so I couldn't call Ang and tell her I was ok. I ended up getting in the shower and going to sleep. Being with Zaire, those few days; he wouldn't let me shower and only made sure I ate and used the bathroom. Shit, I felt like a filthy animal. I thought about waking my grandparents up and let them know, I'm here but its late. I would speak to them tomorrow. Right now, I was too exhausted and tired, to speak to anyone.

****

"GET OUT OF MY HOUSE CARA! YOU'VE DONE NOTHING BUT CAUSE PROBLEMS WITHIN THIS FAMILY." I heard my grandmother yelling downstairs. I sat up and listened.

"Why are you always protecting her? I'm your granddaughter too." I made my way to the top of the steps by now, to listen.

"Cara, you've been nothing but horrible to her, since you were kids."

"Grandma, you and grandpa, were mean to her too."

"See it how you want but it was for her own good."

"Her own good, huh?"

"Yes, because we knew being a baby addicted to drugs, would have an effect on her in the future. I don't expect you to understand because you had your mother around and didn't

22

have to deal with the trials and tribulations, she did. Rakia, isn't retarded or special because she has anxiety issues but you made her feel like she was and for what? To be the popular girl, or embarrass her to get laughs. The sad part is, you've been mean to her for so long, I doubt you would even know how to stop, if you tried." I could hear her suck her teeth.

"I don't know why you treated her differently, when you're as beautiful as, she is. Honey, you and Rakia, were both blessed with bodies and faces to die for. You had every opportunity as her, to go to school and do whatever she did. What is about her, that you hate so much?" It was silence.

"Then you go and try to cash a check, I'd been saving for her since birth and got caught." My mouth hit the floor. I knew the check was missing but had no idea, she was the reason why.

"Whatever grandma."

"Don't whatever me. I called her over here that day, to have you all get along and the first thing you do is, cause a scene over a truck, her man purchased for her."

"That's not her man. He's mine. Why does everyone keep saying that?"

"Child, you're crazy." I could picture my grandmother walking away from her.

"I saw him first." I shook my head, listening to her lie.

"No, you didn't. That man came over here and told us, everything that really happened at the bodega."

"So, he mentioned New York."

"Yes, he did. He told me, it was nothing more than you giving him oral sex and whatever happened the night of his party, is because you crept into his home, with some other chick he was sleeping with. He kicked you out and then beat you up for trying to hurt Rakia. Honey, what is it about the man, that has you going crazy over him?"

The night of his party? What was she doing at his house? I thought he left with Bobbi. Cara said, he beat her up again but never why he did it. Whatever happened, is the reason my aunt attacked me. I had to find out what went down because maybe it'll explain a lot.

"I'm in love with him grandma."

"And he's in love with Rakia." I smiled, listening to her say he loved me but it vanished quickly with her next statement.

"He won't be for long. I'm gonna make sure, she suffers a horrible fate."

SMACK! SMACK! I heard and my grandfather started yelling at Cara.

"How dare you wish death on her?" He yelled and I ran in my room, to look out the window. My grandfather was going off on her, on the porch. Instead of listening any longer, I hopped in the shower, got dressed and went downstairs.

"RAKIA! When did you get here?" My grandfather yelled and my grandmother turned around with tears in her eyes. I ran to the front door, locked it and then put the window down in the kitchen.

"Why are you locking everything up?"

"I don't want anyone to find me, not even him."

"Honey, he was going crazy last night trying to figure out who had taken you." I grabbed a bowl and poured me some cereal.

25

"I'll give you the money for eating the food." She waved me off.

"Grandma, he doesn't care about me like he says." I explained everything and she shook her head.

"I really liked him for you Rak. I'm not saying, throw away whatever you had but you should see him and find out why he hung up on the guy. The phone could've been disconnected because he lost service, or maybe he was gonna find you on his own." I thought about what she said and it could be possible. I'm not gonna worry myself over it right now.

"Grandma, please don't tell anyone I'm here. I'll pay you for food and to stay here."

"Rakia, I don't wanna lie."

"Grandma, just don't tell him or anyone else, anything." She finally agreed and I asked her to call my cousin Rahmel over. I know he wouldn't say anything and I needed him to grab me a few things. My clothes and other things were here, so that wasn't gonna be an issue.

****

"What up grandma?" I heard and went downstairs.

"Oh shit. Yo, that nigga looking hard as hell for you. Let me call him and get my reward."

"Reward?"

"Yea, he offered 25k to anyone who saw you." He lifted his phone up.

"Don't." I grabbed his hand and took him upstairs but not without noticing my grandmother, giving me a hateful look. As you can tell, she loves Marco but in my eyes, he was no longer my savior.

"Why you hiding out?"

"Look Rahmel, I need you to do me a favor." He sat on the bed and flipped through the channels.

"What?"

"Grandma, isn't happy about me staying here?"

"Why?"

"She doesn't wanna lie to him, if he comes here to search again. Can I stay at your place, pleaseeeeeeeee?" I whined and pouted.

"Mannnnn."

27

"Come on, Rahmel. You have a two bedroom and live out in the boondocks. No one even knows where you live. I won't bother you and I'll pay you."

"How the hell you gonna pay me?" I pulled out the rest of the money, I had left over from Marco. I was going to give it to my grandma but she wasn't beat to have me there. He blew his breath out.

"Fine, but I don't want your money."

"Why not?"

"Because you're family and I know, if the tables were turned, you'd do it for me. However, we have to play this off, to get you out the house."

"What you mean?"

"Make a plan because grandma won't lie for you. We both know that. I'm gonna leave and yell up the steps, how I'm gonna tell him where you are. Tonight, I'll throw a rock at the window, to let you know to come outside and we'll go from there. I don't wanna take any chances of the nigga and his goons, seeing us. I love you to death but I'm not tryna die over you either." I agreed and understood.

28

He left a few minutes later, yelling up the steps, about how he was telling where I was and I better not leave this house. My grandma must've believed him because she sure came up and asked, why won't I call him on my own. I tried to explain my reasons but she kept yelling and slammed my door on the way out.

I stayed in my room all day and packed two duffle bags. One had clothes in them and the other had my underclothes and pajamas. I placed a pair of sneakers and slippers in a shopping bag and tied it to one of the duffles. It wasn't until after midnight, when Rahmel came to get me. I left my grandma a note, saying I was leaving because no one wanted to help me and its time to figure it out on my own. I left it on the bed, tiptoed down the steps and out the back door. At this moment, I loved that my grandparents slept with the fan and AC on. They couldn't hear a thing and its exactly, what I needed.

Rahmel and I walked through the backyard and ended up on the other street. His car was still running. He helped me put the bags in the car and we drove off. I laid the seat all the way back, so no one would see me as his passenger and fell asleep on the way. He shook me when we got there and helped me take my stuff out. Thank goodness, there were only a few houses on his street and every light in their homes were out. My cousin loved to live in peace, which is why, he left my aunt years ago. We walked up the steps and as he unlocked the door, I kept looking behind me, thinking Marco or someone would pop out.

I followed him in the house and smiled. He had a bachelor's pad and I noticed all the grocery bags on the table, full of boxed and canned food. He told me, he put the cold stuff away before he came. I went to the room he had for me and noticed a brand-new comforter set on the side of the bed, new towels, feminine hygiene stuff and morning hygiene products. I asked who got all this, he said, his chick works at target and he told her, his twelve-year-old cousin, was coming to stay for a while. He couldn't have her sleeping in a guy, type of room, which explains the pink comforter set. I wasn't complaining because it was the thought that counts.

"I left some chicken out so after you're done, I expect something to eat."

"Boy!"

"Nah, man. You had me paranoid all day getting this spot ready for you. The least you can do, is cook your favorite cousin a meal." He walked away and left me standing there.

Instead of unpacking, I took the comforter set out the bag and placed it in the washer. I hated the smell of new items from the store and always had to clean them first. I went in the kitchen, took the chicken out, cleaned, seasoned it and turned the oil on to get ready, to cook. My grandmother may have been mean but she taught me how to cook and damn good, I may add. I put the rest of the groceries away and waited for the grease to get hot. Once it did, I dipped the chicken in flour and let it fry.

By the time, I finished cooking, it was almost two in the morning. We were both starving and making our plates, when his phone rang. It scared the daylights outta me. He told me, that's why I needed to let Marco, know where I was because I wouldn't be so jumpy. It must've been his girl because he told her, he loved her and would see her tomorrow. He hung up and sat down with me in the kitchen.

"You know, you'll eventually have to show your face." He said and grabbed the hot sauce.

"I know. Right now, I want a break from everything and everybody."

"Listen cuz. I understand why you feel the way you do but you're almost twenty years old. This running away shit, is for teenagers. It may hurt but it's time to be a grown up and deal with shit, like one."

"I don't know how. Rahmel, I've never been with a man and the first one, I fall in love with, cheats on me, or should I say, actually listened, when I said stay away from me, and had sex with another woman. Then he saved me from your mom's attack, only to leave me hanging, when someone kidnaps me. Love isn't my expertise and I keep messing up because I don't know what I'm doing." I dropped the fork and broke down crying. He rubbed my back and slid my hair behind my ear.

"No one is an expertise in this love game. Rak, everyone messes up and it happens a lot, until they get it right. He knows the type of person you are and still loves you." I looked up.

"I don't know why he hung up, or didn't come to your rescue but the fact is; you're safe and won't call him."

"Why would I? He obviously doesn't wanna see me." I picked my fork up and started playing with my macaroni and cheese.

"Ugh, because he has a damn reward out for you."

"It could be to kill me. You do know he's dangerous."

"Rak, he's not the type of nigga to make people think, he wants to kill them. He just does it. No one is to touch you, if they found you. He told everyone to call him and he'd handle it from there." I sipped on my soda.

"I'll call him in a few days. Can you give me that?"

"I'm not gonna pressure you to do anything. If you love him like you claim, you'll start missing him and want to on your own."

"I already do."

"Well then, you know what to do." He handed me his phone and I took it in the room.

"RAHMEL!" I screamed and he came running.

"WHAT?" I started laughing at how nervous he was.

"I'm sorry. How do you block the number to call someone? I don't want him to see where I'm calling from and come after you."

"Good idea." He did it for me and left out the room. I heard the phone ring and got nervous, each time it kept ringing. Just as I was about to hang up, he answered. It sounded like he was asleep. I blew my breath. *Here goes nothing.*

Marco

"Hello." The number was blocked, which let me know it was Rak. I only know that because, I had word the dude, Z was back in Connecticut and he had no need to contact me, if they weren't together.

I found out he was the one who had her, when he sent me the video of them fucking. I'm still not sure, what the affiliation between the two of them were but I will soon. Then his dumb ass, had the nerve to contact me about having her. I hung up because if he was fucking her, why would he try and pretend he would hurt her? It obvious, he was enjoying himself. Any ransom he was asking for, would be for them to live off of and I'll be damned if she lived her days with some other nigga, off my dime. I don't care how anyone looks at it.

"Marco."

"What Rak?" I sat up in the bed.

"I miss you."

"Is that all you called me for?"

"Ugh ok. Why do you have a reward out for me, if you hung the phone up on the guy who called to get a ransom?" See, this the shit I'm talking about. Why ask me about not paying, instead of telling me why, the two of them thought they would scam me?

"Because I'm gonna kill you, for tryna play me."

"Whyyyy. Wouldddddd. You kill me, Marco?" I smiled. Not because of her being nervous but the way she stuttered. She was scared and I could still hear the love, she had for me in her voice.

"Why not? You fucked that nigga Rak. After all the shit you talked, you go and cheat on me. What the fuck is going on? You weren't happy? What was it?" Hell yea, I was in my feelings a little. I was in love with her and she went out and allowed another nigga to touch her. And before anyone talks shit, we weren't a couple the two times, I slept with those women. She told me to leave her alone, each time.

"Marco, he.-"

"He sent me the video Rakia, so don't deny it." I was standing up, pacing the floor in my room because of how mad, she got me.

"I wasn't."

"WHAT?" I was enraged, that she admitted to it.

"It's not what you think and I'm sorry, you had to see me with another man but that's what you get." When the hell did she become bold?

"What the fuck you say?" I started putting my clothes on. Rak, had me ready to go out and find her.

"I said, it's what you get. Now you see, how I felt opening the car door and witnessing you, plunge your dick, in another woman." I couldn't say shit.

"You know, the type of person I am, when it comes to my privacy. It wasn't intentional to hurt you but now that you've seen it, there's nothing I can do about it."

"So, you tough now? That nigga got you talking out the side of your neck, huh?"

"No, I'm not tough and he's nowhere around. However, I don't appreciate you wanting to kill me, for seeing me do,

37

what you did. The situations were totally different and if you asked, I would've told you, he taped me in school not too long ago without my knowledge. He did a lot of other things to me too Marco, that I didn't consent to but you could care less, right?" *Is she telling me he raped her?*

"As long as, you can kill me for hurting you, nothing else matters. Forget how many times you hurt me." I heard so much anger and hurt in her voice and the shit was killing me. We may not have been an official couple but the things I did, hurt her and I've been tryna make up for them, ever since. Unfortunately, the nigga snatched her up and sent me this so-called, old video. Old or not, I'm still pissed she slept with someone else.

"Rak."

"No Marco. I left school to get away from him. He sends you an old video and you automatically believe, I'd do you dirty. You did the same thing, when the Bobbi girl told you about our baby. You always jump to conclusions; never giving me the chance to explain and then find a way to hurt me. He called for you to save me and you hung up because you

38

were mad. Well guess what? Maybe, if you kill me, he won't be able to find me again and call you, to save me, just to hang up. I hate you Marco." She said and the phone disconnected. I couldn't even call her back because the number was blocked. In order for me to get it, I needed her to stay on the phone for another forty seconds. *FUCK!!!*

****

"Where is she?" I asked Rakia's grandmother when she opened the door.

"I don't know. She was here last night and I told her, to call you but she kept saying no. Then Cara, came over talking about how in love with you, she was. I told her, you were in love with Rakia and she said not for long. Marco, you have to find her. I think, Cara wants to kill her. Please don't let that happen."

"Where's Cara?" This bitch is a pain in my ass and it time to get rid of her. Rak, can be mad but the bitch is causing way too much drama for one person. I could tell how tired their grandmother is and it seems like she wants me to anyway.

39

"Who knows? Her and Shanta, haven't been staying home so I couldn't tell you, even if I wanted to." I gave her a hug and left to go see Tech, at the hospital.

The other night, someone sprayed the cop car, killing the officer and almost killed Ang. She was in a coma as of right now and Tech wasn't taking it well. We had no idea who did it, or why anyone would want her dead. Ang, didn't have enemies either; therefore, we couldn't figure it out. One would believe it to be Cara but she was at the house still, when we left so it wasn't her. Plus, whoever did it, had a machine gun, which means, they knew exactly, what they were doing.

Most of the bullets were embedded in the doors but a few got through the window, which is how the officer, was shot in the head. They said he died instantly, so the crash didn't affect him at all. Evidently, once he was hit, he ran into a telephone pole and flew through the windshield. When they found Ang, she was lying down in the back seat but with a few bullet holes in her body. One hit her in the shoulder and another one, in her thigh. It caused a rupture in one of her major arteries. They had to put her in a coma because of the

40

head trauma. When the car hit the pole, she must've banged her head on the door really hard. She had swelling on her brain and they wanted to make sure she didn't have seizures, or some shit.

I parked in the visitors' section and took one of the passes from the reception desk. I pressed the elevator to get on the ICU floor and saw Ang's father and my godson, sitting in the waiting area. I asked why and he said, the nurse was cleaning her up. Her mom and Tech, were in there to make sure, no funny shit went down. I would've done the same thing. I sat down and picked lil Antoine up. He seemed to be growing overnight and his ass was chunky as hell. I don't know what the hell they were feeding him but he needed to be on a damn diet.

"Marco, can you go check on him?" Ang's mom said, when she came out in the waiting room.

"What's up?" I handed the baby to her.

"The nurse was washing her up and the monitors were going off. He thought something was wrong and security had to come up here. You know how he is over her." I nodded and went right in. She was right about Tech. He was crazy in love with Ang and if he thought for one minute, something was suspect, he'd flip. I could hear him yelling as I walked to her room.

"I got it." Security looked at me and then him.

"I said, I got it. We good." Tech was breathing heavy and ready to kill someone. I pushed him in the room and closed the door. Besides the bandage on her head, Ang, looked like she was asleep.

"What happened?"

"I didn't like how rough the bitch was being with her and Ang, didn't either because her monitors started beeping and her heartrate was increasing. They tried to tell me it was normal. If that's the case, the other woman who's been washing her, ain't never had an issue. I'm far from stupid. The bitch was being rough on purpose and I told her, if she ever stepped foot in this room again, I'll break her fucking neck. Her dumb ass called security." He kissed Ang on the lips and sat down.

"What's good with you? You find Rak, yet?"

"Nah, but she called and I fucked up." He gave me the side eye. I told him what happened and he shook his head.

"So, the nigga is the reason she came home and you left her to fend for herself, because you were mad. Bro, I thought, I had it bad."

"Fuck you, nigga. I have to find her and apologize. Oh, and Cara, wants Rakia dead because in her head with Rakia, gone, I'll run to her. I can't tell you who's crazier between her and Bobbi but both of those bitches, are looney as fuck."

"You did it."

"What the fuck ever. They should know to move on, if a nigga don't want them. Shit, Cara only got the dick once and that was recently. She's been acting crazy, from just sucking it."

"At least, she's bothering you."

"Nah. What the fuck were you thinking by paying the bitch to keep quiet?"

"Nigga, I ain't pay the bitch shit. She said all that, to get Ang mad. I wish, I would pay her to keep quiet about something between us, way before Ang and I, ever spoke.

You're right about one thing and that's, that she's delusional and has to go. She fucked up by lying to Ang and if you don't find her before me, I'll make sure she suffers for you too." I nodded and the two of us sat there watching the baseball game on television. My phone went off and it was a message from Bobbi. I opened it and showed Tech. *This bitch is still trying.* I kissed Ang on the cheek and told him, I'd be back, later or tomorrow.

"He's good. Whoever the nurse was, isn't allowed back in there. So, make sure the doctors know it, or it won't be good next time." Her parents thanked me and I left. I had to make a few stops and the first one, is to this bitch's house.

****

"I had to send you an ultrasound photo, to get you here?" She stepped aside for me to come in.

"You and I, both know you're not pregnant and if you are, it ain't mine." She sucked her teeth and followed me in the living room.

I plopped down on her couch and asked what she wanted. I sent a message to one of the guys at the warehouse to

44

make sure, shit was right until I got there. I ended up scrolling through my photos and came across a few of Rak. She would kill me if she knew, I even had these. There was one of her asleep in the bed and one in her bra and panty set. I caught it when she wasn't paying attention. Another one, she had just gotten out the bathroom and only had on a towel. Her hair was soaking wet and clinging to her face. I had to put my phone up because the pictures were getting me aroused and this is not the place, for it to happen at.

"If you know that, why did you come?" She asked and stood in front of me.

"I came to tell you to stop hitting my line. I told you it was over. Then you starting with this bullshit, ultrasound photo."

"Marco, you know, you still want this." She took her shirt off. Bobbi, was pretty with a banging body to match but she wasn't for me.

"Move." I pushed her out the way and stood up.

"So, you telling me, you're really in love with this retard?" I stopped walking to the door and turned around. She knew nothing about Rak, which told me, Cara and her, have been conversing about my girl.

"Don't ever speak about my girl like that." I mushed her so hard, she hit her head on the wall.

"Marco, let me be your side chick. You know, I won't say anything."

"Are you crazy? My woman, doesn't deserve me to cheat on her for some community pussy or any other kind. She has my heart shorty and there's nothing you, her cousin or any other woman can do, to make me cheat on her."

"Not even me." I heard the voice and refused to turn around. If I did, I couldn't tell you what would happen. What the fuck was Mia, even doing here? Was this a setup the entire time? I headed to the door and heard her, walking behind me.

Mia, was the love of my life, when I was fourteen. She was my first at everything; including sex and my first heartbreak. She and I, met as freshman and were together, up until prom night.

I picked her up and all I could think of, was taking her to the hotel and sexing her all night afterwards. Yea, we had sex before plenty of times but they always say prom night is special. I wanted to experience it and from what she said, she did too. The entire night, we danced, drank some liquor one of the guys snuck in and we even made, prom King and Queen. That's how much people loved us as a couple.

Long story short, it was time to go and I couldn't find Mia, anywhere. The teachers kept telling us to leave but I asked them, could I check one more time. They told me yes, so I ran all around looking. Something told me to look in the classrooms. All of them were locked, except one. I opened the door and Mia, was laid out on a table with her legs on some nigga's shoulders, getting fucked. I slammed the door hard and walked towards them. The glass shattered everywhere but not like my heart did, when I saw who the guy was. It was one of my best friends and I didn't have but two of those. He was one and Tech was the other.

"Really, Dennis? You're fucking my girl." I took my suit jacket off and got ready to square up. Mia, hopped off the table and pulled her dress down. She had the nerve to beg me not to fight him.

"Marco, I'm sorry. We're in love." It was like, the air was knocked outta me, when he said that. How could he be in love with my girl and then he said, she felt the same.

"Is this true Mia?" She nodded her head yes.

"You know what? Ain't no need to even fight you over her. But Mia, you." I pushed her against the wall.

"Stop Marco. She's pregnant." I backed away and stared at her. I knew for a fact; the kid wasn't mine because we always used condoms. I was too young for a kid and had plans to build my own empire. It would require a lot of time outta the house and I didn't wanna neglect my kid or girl, in the process.

"You two are dead to me."

"Marco, I'm sorry. It happened one night we were drunk and never stopped. We never meant to hurt you." Dennis said.

"I'm not hurt, bro." I grabbed my suit jacket and walked out the classroom and building. Tech and his date were waiting in the limo. He must've saw me coming out the school upset, and hopped out the car.

"What happened?"

48

"Take me home bro." He didn't ask any questions and told the limo driver to drop his date off and then us. That's why he was my nigga. The chick he took to prom, promised to do all this freaky shit to him and he couldn't wait. But he pushed her to the side, to be there for me, which is why, he's my partner. Fuck that; my brother.

"Dennis and Mia, have been fucking and she's pregnant by him."

"WHAT THE FUCK? I HOPE YOU BEAT HIS ASS AND SLID HER ACROSS THE FLOOR OR SOMETHING." He said.

"I couldn't do it. Mia, was scared to death and Dennis was still my boy."

"Don't tell me, you'll still fuck with him after this."

"Hell no. There's gonna come a time when he'll need me, you wait and see." He nodded and the two of us, got drunk as hell and passed out.

The following Monday in school, these motherfuckers had the nerve, to walk around like a couple. They were throwing the shit in my face and I had to calm myself down a few times, to keep from fucking them up. Shit, I even had to stop Tech from killing him at the bowling alley, one night. How do you grow up as brothers and go behind one of their backs, fuck his girl and get her pregnant? Anyway, after high school, Dennis and his mother moved to Connecticut and has been there ever since. Mia, went a few months later and supposedly, they got married and had the kid.

Low and behold; there was a guy from Connecticut, that went by the name D, who was looking for a new plug, five years ago. Evidently, his got knocked and he needed product fast. I had my guy look into him and wouldn't you know; D and Dennis, were one of the same. I never contacted him, or mentioned, I knew who he was and, I'd be more than happy to supply him.

I over charged the shit outta him and even had his shit watered down, before it was sent to him. I made sure the workers didn't make it noticeable at first and then, gradually let them. He contacted one of the workers, complaining and I had them tell him, he could keep working with me, or find someone new. I guess, this is when he made plans to come for me. Little did he know, we were waiting for the day and set the whole shit up, thanks to his cousin Shana. She was the stripper, Tech fucked, off and on. She told us he called and tried to get her, to get information on us.

Tech gave her some fake shit to see if she'd really tell him and sure enough, she did. It's another reason, why Tech couldn't mess with her on any other level than fucking. She couldn't be trusted. Unfortunately, Dennis, sealed his own fate and I'm the one who took his life. He begged and pleaded for his wife and child. I didn't give a fuck, just like they didn't, when they fucked me over. I told him, karma is a bitch and watched him take his last breath. Now, his wife slash, widow, had the nerve to be following me outside Bobbi's house, begging for me to talk to her. I got in my car and pulled off. *The fucking audacity!*

Tech

As I sit here, staring at my wife in this hospital bed, I couldn't stop thinking about, who could have done this to her? Neither, her or Rakia had enemies, as far as we knew. Well, besides Cara and the two crazy bitches we fucked with; no one comes to mind. But to shoot up a police car is crazy, even for Marco and I. We've done some shit in our life and if it came down to killing a cop, we would but it's never come to it.

I walked up on the scene, after Marco made me get out and saw a body on the stretcher, in a body bag. I didn't wanna believe it was her and made the coroner, unzip the bag. My heart stopped beating for a minute and started back up, when I saw the cop, who put her in his car, in it. I walked up to the ambulance and that's when I saw them placing and IV in her arm. She had blood coming from everywhere. I was about to get in there with her, until I saw Bobbi, standing in the cut. Why the fuck was she here?

I ran after her and started shooting. I could hear Marco, calling my name and people yelling and screaming. I felt, if Bobbi was there and she did it, or knew the person who did, they'd be with her. Unfortunately, I tackled the bitch to the ground and put my gun to her head. She said, she was at her mom's house and heard the shooting and crash. I had to believe her because her mom did live in the area. I stood up and asked Marco to take me to the hospital because I could hear the ambulance going down the street.

It didn't take us any time to get there and once we did, they took her straight in the back. I sat there for hours waiting. I called her pops, explained what happened and by the time they got there with my son, the doctor was just coming out. He took us in a room and explained the areas she was hit and why he had to place her in a coma. My head was all over the place by now and her mom, tried to tell me everything would be ok. However, she didn't see Ang, the way I did.

I've been at the hospital every day and haven't left to get a haircut or anything. Marco, brings clothes up for me and her parents, bring my son to sit with us. He stays for hours with me and I have them pick him up around seven. I like for them to take him home, bathe, feed and have him in bed early. He's still only a couple months old but Ang, has him on this schedule and

I wanna keep it that way.

****

"Good morning, Mr. Miller. How are you today?" The doctor asked.

"I'm good. When is she gonna wake up?"

"Well. We did the MRI yesterday, as you know and the swelling has gone down, tremendously. I had the nurse give her the medication to pull her out of the coma, so basically it's up to her, at this point."

"Is there anything to speed up the process? I want my wife awake."

"I'm sorry but it's not. It could be today, tonight or even tomorrow, when she opens her eyes. Just make sure you're here when she does." He said and walked out after checking her vitals. I grabbed her hand and kissed it.

54

"Ang baby, I know you can hear me. Our son, needs you to wake up. I need you to wake up. I wanna tell you the truth about the Cara bitch. What she told you is partly true but not the full truth. I swear, I never slept with her when we were together. I wouldn't do that to you. Come on baby. I need to make love to you. Please wake up." I wiped the few tears from my eyes and stood up to kiss her lips.

I ended up moving her over a little and got in bed with her. This was my first time doing it and it felt good, lying next to her. I turned on my side and laid my arm on her stomach. I thought one of her fingers moved but when I lifted her hand, nothing happened. I turned the channel to sports center and watched as much as I could. My eyes started closing, so I got as comfortable as I could, in the bed.

"Wake up baby, so I can put my daughter in you." I whispered in her ear and kissed the side of her face. The machine beeped fast for a few seconds and then, back to normal.

"I know you hear me Ang. Find a way to open those eyes. I love you." I closed my eyes and sleep found me in no time.

****

"I see you slept well, Mr. Miller." The doctor said.

"Lying next to me wife, for the first time in weeks, is what did it."

Ang, has been in the hospital now for over a month. Her wounds were almost healed and the swelling on her brain, is gone. They were waiting on her to wake up. The therapist has been in twice a day, to make sure her limbs were mobile and not stiff. It cost a pretty penny to get them there twice a day and seven days a week. Usually, the therapist would come a few times a week. I spared no expense for my wife. She would be determined to get out the bed, once she opened her eyes and I was making sure, it was possible.

"That's great."

"Hey doc. Since she's outta the danger zone, do you think it's possible, I can take her home? Her mom, will be there to help and if I need a nurse, I'll hire one."

"I don't see why not? I mean, it's not something, I'd ever recommend but if you have the money and equipment to take care of her, then I'd say, do it. She's only sleeping at this point."

"Cool. We'll be outta here in an hour."

"Um ok. Let me get the discharge papers ready. I'm gonna give you a number to the VNA, which is a company who sends nurses out to homes. Your wife will need an IV, to feed her body nutrients and keep her hydrated. Otherwise, everything else is ok for her to leave." He walked out and I called Marco.

"Meet me at the hospital in about an hour."

"Everything good?" He questioned.

"Yea. Also, I need you to get the nurse you used to fuck with from here and see if she can stop by too."

"I'm calling her now."

"See you in an hour." The next call was to her parents.

"Do you think it's ok for her to come home?" Her mom asked.

"Yes. Plus, I've been missing my son. He needs to be back in his house, with his parents." I threw that in there because she was starting to act like he was her son. I appreciated the fuck outta them, for taking care him. But he's my son and ain't nobody about to tell me shit about raising him but his mother; my wife.

After I hung up with her, I washed Ang myself and dressed her in a gray sweat suit. Marco's mom, who I considered my own; has come up to visit a few times and brought her some clothes and stuff from the house. I did my best at brushing her hair in a ponytail but the shit still looked crazy. I made one of the nurses come do it for me.

Marco called me in exactly an hour and said, he was here. I told him to park outside and the doctor had someone bring her down in a stretcher. They tried to send her home in an ambulance, but its no need, when me and my brother, can get her in the house. Luckily, there were only a few people in the lobby, so it didn't look crazy bringing her down. He opened the back door to the truck and helped me put her in. I put the seatbelt on and sat next to her so she wouldn't fall over.

58

It's like she was passed out drunk but we all knew it wasn't the case. I made sure to keep her seated correctly on the ride home.

I carried her in the house and laid her in the bed. Her parents came over with my son not too long after and so did the nurse. She set the IV up and said she'd come by tomorrow. I asked what if the IV ran out? She promised it wouldn't because the bag was big and she had it on slow drip. I walked all of them out, kicked it with my son for a few hours, then got him ready for bed. I locked up, jumped in the shower and came out to see my wife staring at me, with tears streaming down her face.

"I'm so happy, you woke up." I dropped to my knees in front of her.

"I'm thirsty." She whispered. I ran down the steps dripping wet, with a towel wrapped around me. I grabbed a water bottle, a cup and ran back upstairs. She was trying to sit up.

"Hold on." I helped her and poured some water in the cup.

"How you feel?"

"I don't really know." She ran her hand down my face and then slapped the shit out of me. It stung like hell but I know she's been waiting to do it, since hearing about the shit with Cara.

"Why?"

"Ang, three weeks before we exchanged numbers, Cara was at the club. I asked her for your number and she gave me a hard time. Even then, she was hating on you. Anyway, I walked her to the bathroom and shit happened in there. I had to stop because she couldn't take the dick. I never touched her again, which is why she was talking shit at the block party."

"But you paid here."

"Lies." I shook my head.

"I ain't pay that bitch shit. I'm not gonna lie though, she did try and pull some stunt, that if I didn't, she'd tell. I called her bluff and she did it anyway. I should've told you but I wasn't tryna to lose you."

"It was before me but Tech, I don't fuck after her." I knew she'd say that, which is exactly why, her ass stayed in the dark about it.

60

"Ang, I'm sorry for not telling you and giving her the upper hand to hurt you. I swear, on my son, the two of us haven't been sexually active in any way."

"Do you know the reason why I hit her?" I stood up to put some boxers on. I told her not to speak too much but she wanted to tell me.

"You should've stomped her out."

"I fought her for bothering Rakia. Then, she called the cops on me and said, for me not to worry about you because she'd handle you like before. All I saw was red and unfortunately, the cops were right there. Oh my God, is the cop ok?"

"He didn't make it Ang." She started crying.

"Who would do something like that? Baby, I don't bother anyone. Do I have to look over my shoulder now? Wait! Where's my son?" I walked out the room, went to get him and brought him to her.

"I missed you so much." She kissed all over him and laid him on her chest. He squirmed a little and then got comfortable. I swear, he knew his mom was holding him.

"Tech, I heard you crying and cursing people out. I missed you too. If I could've woke up for you and my son, I would have. I tried so many times to open my eyes but I couldn't. I feared, years would go by and I wouldn't know my son and you'd find someone else." She started crying again. I took my son and laid him on the bed.

"Ang, you're not my girlfriend anymore. You're my wife, my best friend and my other half. I would never leave you, or find someone else because you're outta commission. You and my son mean the world to me and I'm in this, til death do us part. Even then, I'm coming to find you." She smiled and I kissed her lips.

"You're too sexy for me to leave and you know, I'm hooked on you."

"I'm hooked on you too. Can you start a bath for me?" I stood up and did what she asked. I undressed, carried and placed her in the tub, gently.

"Can you get in with me?" It didn't matter I just showered. If my wife wanted to be close with me behind her, then that's what she's gonna get. I put my son back in his crib and stepped in with her.

"Don't sit yet." I stood there confused. She had me stand in front of her as she fixed herself. She was face to face with my dick and let's just say, she gave me what I've been needing for a month now.

"Fuck sitting in here. I'm washing you up. I need to taste you."

"It's ok Antoine." I smirked. She barely ever calls me that.

"Maybe for you it is but not me. My wife has to get hers too." She shook her head laughing. I washed both of us up and did exactly what I said. I was holding off on sex, though. She may be awake but my wife likes to be in control too.

Angela

"Yes baby, yesssssss." I moaned out as Tech, hit my spot over and over. I've been awake now for three weeks and I swear, we've been making up ever since. He didn't want to at first but after the first few days, a bitch needed it. He was walking around the house with no shirt on, or coming out the shower dripping wet. There's no way, I could allow him to continue, without touching.

"You like this." He went deeper.

"Baby, I'm gonna cummmmmmmm." I let my juices coat his dick.

"Damn, that's a lot, Ang." He lifted me up and had me ride him. This is actually the first time, since opening my eyes. I could've done it but my legs were still weak at the time. He put me on top and both of us, moaned out. I grinded my hips and he sat up to watch.

"Just like that. Shit, you feel good. Mmmmm. Damn, I missed this." He smacked me on the ass a few times and it was on from there. We had sex most of the night, until my son woke up hungry.

"I got him." I said and ran in the bathroom to wipe up and then take care of him. I came out and Tech was lying on his stomach, trying to go to sleep. I shook my head and walked out.

"Hey, mommy's baby." I lifted him up and went downstairs to get his bottle. As I waited, for it to heat up, I heard a phone vibrating. I looked and it was mine, thank goodness. I don't think I could take, another woman calling him.

I glanced at the number and had no idea, who it was. I put it back down and it rang again. Usually, I wouldn't answer it but something told me to. I was hoping it was Rakia because from what Tech told me; no one has seen or heard from her, since the night, the Zaire guy took her. She called Marco after Zaire, left her on the street and he basically blacked out, made plans to kill her and then felt bad, once he heard the truth. I don't blame her for saying she hated him. I'm sure, she doesn't but the fact she said it, fucked Marco up. That's what he gets, if you ask me.

"Hello."

"Oh my God! Ang, you're ok. How are you? I'm so sorry, I couldn't see you." She started rambling. I picked my son's bottle up and took him in the living room. I turned the television on and got him comfortable on my lap.

"Where are you? And, are you ok?" I asked and she blew her breath out. I knew she didn't wanna tell me where she was, just by the sound of her sighing.

"Ang, please don't tell anyone, where I am."

"You know, I won't."

"I'm at Rahmel's and have been the entire time. Ang, it's so peaceful here. He's barely ever here and I've been doing a lot of work from school."

"What you mean?"

"I contacted my school and they allowed me to take online courses for the summer. It will help me graduate faster too."

"I'm proud of you Rak." My son started crying.

"Let me go. I'm gonna call you in the morning. We're going out to eat. Your godson, misses you."

"Awwww. I miss him too."

"Rak, I promise not to tell anyone, where you are."

"K. I can't wait to see you two tomorrow." I hung the phone up and stood to go upstairs.

"How is she?" Tech asked and took my son.

"I won't be able to tell, until I'm around her." He nodded and took my hand to go upstairs.

"I'm going to lunch with her tomorrow."

"Where?" He asked and I didn't answer.

"Tech, she doesn't wanna see him and as her friend, it's only fair, that we respect her wishes."

"Ang, you know he wants to apologize and make sure she's good." We got in the bed and laid my son in the middle.

"I know but let me see where her head is first. If Marco, didn't wanna see her, you wouldn't tell her where he was; now would you?"

"Probably not."

"Exactly! Let me see if I can at least get her to call him again. But I'm not making promises and don't have anyone following me."

"You out your rabid ass mind, if you think for one minute, I won't have someone watching you, after what happened."

"Fine! But if he shows up, I promise to give you the silent treatment and you know, pussy is definitely off the menu." He sucked his teeth.

"I'm serious Tech."

"Alright man, damn. I won't mention it but you will have someone following you. And, you better answer when I call, or we both showing up."

"I promise." I leaned over and kissed his lips. I hope Rakia is sure she doesn't wanna be with Marco because he doesn't seem to wanna let her go.

****

"He is so chunky." Rakia said taking lil man out the car seat. We met at one of the diners outside of town.

"Ugh ahh, heffa. Don't come for my baby." I gave her a hug and we walked in to sit. The waitress came right over and took our order. I wasted no time prying.

"So, tell me everything." She started from the moment Zaire took her, all the way up to when she contacted Marco on the phone. I laughed at the way she described everything. She was so proper, which is why, it made me laugh.

"I'm gonna be straight with you Rak." She sucked her teeth. I've always told her, I'd never sugar coat shit and I'm not about to.

"First… you were wrong for not informing him of Zaire, contacting you in the first place." She tried to interrupt me and I told her to wait.

"The man was threatening you over the phone and after what you said he did to you, there's absolutely no reason, Marco wasn't informed. As your man, you know he would've handled it immediately." She nodded.

"Second… I understand you're upset, he hung the phone up but did you look at it from his point?"

"Huh?"

69

"He probably thought, you went willingly with this man and were trying to scam him."

"But I wasn't."

"He received a video from a man, you were fucking and sucking and you're missing. Then, he gets a call from a guy, saying he has you and clearly was about to request money or something. I would've hung up too. It looked suspect as hell but if you had told him the truth and Zaire took you, trust me; it would've went differently. Rakia look."

"I'm not saying he should've put a bounty on your head, or went off on you, without knowing the truth first but you kept it from him. How do you think he feels, knowing his woman thinks he can't protect her, if she has a problem? I, honestly think, the two of you, need to have a talk and if you still don't want him afterwards, that's something to discuss as well. But you hiding out and shit, is for teenagers. Sis, you just turned twenty a week ago. It's time to be an adult." She started crying but it was the truth. She can't keep running away because the problems will still be there, when she comes back.

"I don't know how to be an adult, when it comes to relationships. I know, I keep saying it but it's the truth. I messed up with Zaire and Marco."

"Rakia, you didn't mess up with Zaire, so don't ever let me hear you say that. The two situations are totally different and you needed to get away from him. He's a rapist in my eyes and should be handled accordingly. As far as, Marco, both of you messed up, however, the love is there and neither of you can deny it."

"I told him, I hated him."

"Girl, please. He knows you didn't mean it. Tech, told me he wants to apologize and I think it's the perfect time for you two, to converse."

"I don't know."

"I'm sure you're scared but it's time to grow up. This is your first experience with a guy, so it's expected to be nervous about it. But in order to get better, you have to work on it." She agreed and the two of us, stayed there for another hour talking about everything else.

Once she helped me put my son in the car, I nodded to the guard, I was ready to go home. He started his truck and I could see him in my rearview mirror. I pressed the Bluetooth to answer for Tech. He was checking to make sure, I was ok and on my way home. He had to go somewhere with Marco and wouldn't be home, when I got there. I glanced in my rearview mirror again and someone had clearly cut the guard off.

"Tech, someone is following me." I could see the guard trying to get back in front of them.

"How's that possible?"

"Someone cut the guard off. He's trying to get back in front of him. Oh my God, they hit the back of my car." I yelled out as my neck jerked forward.

"Fuck! Where are you?"

"Techhhhh." I yelled out, as I saw the car coming at fast speed.

"Baby, tell me you're ok. Fuck!" The car hit me so hard from the back, I spun around and hit the side of another car. Whoever was in the car, tried to hit me again on the side, when the guard rammed into their car.

72

"You ok." I heard someone ask. I must've blacked out because I don't remember, opening the car door.

"Check my son." I felt a little blood leaking down my head. My son was hysterical screaming and it only pissed me off more. I tried to get up and fell back in the seat.

"Stay in the seat. Here is your son." A woman passed him to me and kneeled down in front of me.

"Someone tell me where she is, please." I could still hear Tech, coming through the Bluetooth. The woman told him and he pulled up with Marco at the same time, the ambulance came. My car was totaled and so was the person's, who I hit. I glanced around for the other car, and it was turned upside down. I pointed to Tech and the two of them walked over there. I don't know what they were talking about and right now, and I didn't care. I needed to get me and my son, to a hospital.

It took them four hours to fully exam, my son and I. The person in the other car was there too. Tech, went and got their information. He promised to call them tomorrow and get them a brand-new car. He told them they could sue the insurance company for money because he wasn't paying them shit. The poor man, looked scared to death.

He told me the one who actually hit me, is a guy and he was deceased from the impact of the guards' car. I could care less. Death was too easy, for someone who almost killed me and my son. I don't know who's trying to kill me but I hope Tech finds out soon, or I'll never leave the house again.

Cara

I was receiving good news for the last few days and a bitch was happy. First, I heard Rakia disappeared after the shit over my grandmothers and that's been two months now. Then two weeks ago, someone chased Angela down and almost killed her. Marco, no longer wanted anything to do with Bobbi, yet, his ex was in town and trying to win him back. Evidently, she cheated on him years ago, when they were in high school. She left with the guy, he was murdered and now she wants Marco. The shit, is pretty comical to me.

Last night, Bobbi came in the house all late and cursing about something. Yea, I've been shacking up with her, so Tech and Marco, don't find me. Marco, won't kill me because he knows, how bad it would hurt Rakia but I'm sure he'll torture the hell outta me. Tech, on the other hand won't give two fucks about my cousins' feelings and will execute me on sight.

He needs to get over it. Shit, not only did his wife almost die the night someone shot the police car up, at least his skeleton with me was out. I'm not even sure, if they're together because besides the person running her off the road, no one has seen her.

Anyway, Bobbi came in mad as hell and thought she was gonna take it out on my pussy. NOT! She and I have been sleeping with each other and yes, it's been very good but I still won't go down on her. I will fuck the hell outta her, with a strap on though. Now, I see why men love to hit it from the back. You can control a woman's entire being, that way. Bobbi, moans so loud, it turns me on and I can cum off that alone. I definitely stopped her from trying to fuck me, though. Only Marco, can stick his dick in me.

"What you thinking about?" She asked as we walked in Target.

"Nothing really." We went over to the tissue aisle. She said, she'd be back because she wanted to get a certain candle. I don't know why she didn't wait for me.

"Hey, Cara." This chick my brother was fucking, named Missy, spoke. I didn't really rock with her but I always said hello, if she were around.

76

"Hey." I said dryly.

"How's your cousin doing?"

"My cousin Rakia?" I questioned because that's the only person she could be speaking of. My grandmother only had two kids.

"Is that her name?"

"Why you asking about her?"

"Oh, because Rahmel said, his cousin has been staying with him. He doesn't want me to meet her because he claims, she's a piece of work. I've been picking things up for her, since she's only twelve. You know, he's not gonna do it."

"What kind of stuff?" She went down a list of things, starting with a comforter and the list went on.

I smirked because all she did was inform me, of where Rakia was. I spoke to her for a few more minutes and went to find Bobbi. Now, I have two choices. One… is to tell her where Rakia is and we go over there and whoop her ass. Or, go over there and threaten her, to leave Marco alone. I think, I'd rather go with the latter and if I want her ass whooped, I can do it myself.

I found Bobbi and told her, we had to go because my mom, wanted to see me. She knew Shanta was staying with Marco's dad, so he wouldn't find her. At first, I called her stupid because he'd be able to find her there but she said the father, makes it seem like he doesn't know where she is. If she wants to risk her life, then so be it. I'm staying outta sight.

After, I dropped Bobbi off, I made my way to my brother's house. He lived in the boondocks, which is probably why she came out here. I'm not worried about him being here, because he's a mechanic and works all day. Don't ask me how he has a job, with all the weed he smokes. Sometimes, I think he wakes up high.

I got out the car and looked around for what house could be his. I've only been here a few times and I hated it because it was far and all the homes looked alike. I noticed an old woman watering her lawn and walked over to ask if she knew which one he lived in. She pointed to the house, a few doors down from hers. I had the most wicked smile on my face. I knocked on the door and the look of fear on Rakia's face, made my whole day. I pushed past her and went inside. As usual, her geeky ass, had the computer on and books laid out in the living room.

The house was nicer than before, which meant he upgraded, since the last time, I was here. The sectional was gorgeous and so was the big ass television on the wall. The dining room set, went with it and I was mad jealous looking in the room, she occupied. There was a queen-sized canopy bedroom set and she had it laid out. How the fuck he taking care of her and not me? I'm his fucking sister. You bet, I have an issue with it.

"What Cara?" You damn right, I called his ass up.

"How the fuck you over here taking care, of this bitch and I'm your sister."

"Cara, you better not be at my house."

"Why not? You got this slut here."

"Get the fuck out, NOW!" He shouted and I hung up on him. I could hear another phone ring, which meant he was probably calling her. I stood at the top of the steps.

"I don't know Rahmel but she's here." She said.

"Ok. I will tell her to leave but what if she doesn't?"

Nothing else was said, so I went downstairs. She was standing at the door.

"Rahmel, told me to make you leave. He doesn't want you here." I walked in the kitchen, grabbed a bottle of soda and plopped down on the couch. She blew her breath and went to grab her phone but I got to it first.

"What do you want Cara?" She had her arms folded.

"I want you to leave Marco alone."

"I haven't spoken to him, in two months. If you want him, be my guest." I thought she was lying, until I looked in her phone and noticed his name was missing. There were no pictures, contacts or anything pertaining to him. Maybe she was telling the truth, or she knew his number by heart.

"Why do you want him so bad?"

"You're not woman enough for him. He needs me and we both know it." She shook her head, walked over to the couch and picked her laptop up. I snatched it out her hand and tossed it across the room. The shit cracked in half. She ran over to it, to try and fix it. I'm well aware of how much the Apple laptop is, so her crying over it, is expected. I walked over to her and spoke directly in her ear.

"This is my last time telling you. Leave him the fuck alone, or I'm gonna kill you." I pulled the razor out my pocket and cut the side of her neck, the same way, Marco cut me. I also, sliced the entire side of her arm.

"AHHHHHH." She screamed out. I'm not sure, it went as deep for her to need stiches, but blood was definitely pouring out. I ran in the bathroom to see if there was alcohol. When I found some, I came out and poured the shit on her.

"Stop Cara, please. Oh my God, it hurts." She was hysterical crying and lying on the floor.

"Remember what I said." I kicked her in the back and walked out the front door.

I pulled out the parking lot and as I went down the street, I saw two big black trucks going in the direction of my brother's house. I made a U-turn and went back. I parked down the street and ran up to see, if it was, who I thought it was. Sure enough, the door opened and out stepped Marco, Tech and a few other dudes. What the fuck are they doing here? Were they going to kill my brother. I ran back to my car and called him.

"HE'S GOING TO KILL YOU CARA." His voice boomed through the line.

"What?" The way he said it, sent chills down my spine.

"I don't know what you did but he called me, the second he stepped in the house and said, your sisters' dead. What did you do?"

"Nothing, I'm not worried. Rakia, won't let him." He laughed in the phone.

"You don't get it, do you."

"Get what?"

"This time, Rakia can't save you. I've seen him mad Cara but the way he spoke on the phone, was very calm. When you have a maniac like Marco, on the streets, you'd rather him yell, then be calm. I don't know why you always hated her, when all she did was try to love you. You fucked up Cara and no one is going to be able to save you this time. Not Rakia, mom or even grandma. You better run."

"Rahmel, you're gonna let him kill me."

"Cara, I told you for years to leave her alone. You didn't listen. Then, you show up at my place unannounced and did something to her, that triggered his crazy side. You're on your own." He hung up and all of a sudden, I got nervous. I called my mom and told her, I needed to hide out. She gave me an address and told me to meet her there. I didn't wanna stay with her because I felt Marco would find us but if he hasn't found her yet, maybe he won't. One thing, I do know is, I'm going to get Rakia back for opening her mouth, if it's the last thing, I do.

Marco

Tech and I, were on our way outta town, when Rahmel, hit me up, about going to his house. At first, he was nervous about telling me what for but after I barked at him to spit it out, he informed me that Rakia had been staying with him and Cara found her. Yea, I was low key mad but relieved nothing happened to her. I had been looking for her but not really. Once Tech, told me she met up with Ang, I knew she'd call when she was ready to talk. It's how Rak was and I learned that and a whole lot more from her.

We didn't even have to knock on the door because it was open. The entire living room smelled like rubbing alcohol. There was blood dripping on the floor and all I could think of is, Cara either killed, or did some foul shit to Rak.

Tech followed me in the bathroom, where the blood led and Rakia was on the floor, with her knees to her chest crying. There was a towel on her neck and arm. I removed it and lost my fucking mind. I called Rahmel up and told him flat out, his sister is dead. I thought Rak would ask me not to but I think she's had enough.

"Marco, it hurts." She cried in my arms when I lifted her.

"I know ma. I'm taking you to the hospital."

"Do you think she hurt the baby?" I stopped walking and stared at her.

"What baby?"

"I took a test this morning and it was positive. I'm pregnant."

"Rakia."

"It's your baby, Marco. I haven't been with anyone."

"I wasn't going to ask you that." I placed her in the truck. Hell yea, I got that ass pregnant on purpose. When I said her pussy was on lock by me, I meant that shit.

"I was gonna say, there's no more living with other people. I can't protect you, when you're hiding. Ma, this should've never happened."

"I was gonna call you in a few days. Ang, told me you were going out of town and I didn't wanna bother you." I kissed her lips. She was always worried about bothering someone, when she's never one to me.

"When we leave the hospital, I have to go away but I'm gonna have my mom stay with you. I can't leave, knowing you're alone. No one can get in the house but you're pregnant and I want you with someone; in case you need something." She laid her head on my shoulder.

The doctor sent her to the labor and delivery floor and took her right in. They would care for her and the baby up there. I was shocked they let me come in with her but then again, I wouldn't have taken no for an answer. The nurses came in and placed monitors on her stomach and sure enough; my shorty, was having a shorty. You could hear the heartbeat and a nigga, let a tear drop. I had a seed on the way and that shit had me happy as hell; especially, after she got rid of the other one. I don't hold animosity towards her over it because she tried to give me the option, to make the choice with her. Unfortunately, the dumb bitch Bobbi, got in the way. It's all good though because Rakia's about to shit on all these bitches, who hate on her, once I get back from this trip.

After he cleaned the wound, she needed fifteen stitches on her arm and six on her neck. I held her hand the entire time. Each time he stuck the needle in her arm, the monitor would go crazy. They said it was fine but the pain she felt, affected the baby. I almost cursed them out for taking so long. Shit, had my kid and girl in pain, and I wasn't feeling it.

The stupid bitch really tried to slice her up. I'm gonna show her what slicing a motherfucker really is though. I know the one on her neck, is because I did it to her. All Cara did was make me put a hit out on her stupid ass. Money is the root of all evil, so the 50k, I put out, is bound to let me find her soon. It should be easy for me to find her, being who I am, however, I got so, much shit going on with this Zaire dude, I kept putting it on the backburner. Its been a couple of months and there was no sign of her, so I figured she left town. Its not that, I didn't care about Rak but I didn't think Cara would find her. Someone had to have mentioned, where she was.

"Mommy and daddy, do you wanna see your baby?" The doctor asked after the other one, who put the stitches in her arm, left.

"We can?" She was excited and so was I.

"Absolutely. I know you said, you took a test today so let's see when you're due." She smiled and sat in front of some machine.

"Yo, what the fuck is that?" She had this long ass dick, looking thing and tried to put it in Rak's pussy.

"Sir, this is the vaginal ultrasound we give on women, when they first find out about their pregnancy. It gives us an accurate due date."

"Marco, its ok."

"Nah. Can't you use something else?"

"I understand your concern, sir. A lot of daddies have issues with this. If you want to step outside and I'll call you in, after I insert it, we can do that."

"Marco baby, I'm ok. Just stand here and look at me, while she does it. I mean, unless you're not attracted to me anymore." I snapped my neck and looked at her.

"You'll always be attractive to me. Even when my seed blows you up, I'm still gonna love you." I kissed her lips and felt her squeeze my hand, which let me know the doctor, put the thing in.

"Look here. There's your baby." She pointed to the screen and the shit was small. It amazed me, how I could see in her stomach. The baby wasn't big yet but I still saw it.

"Ok, by the ultrasound, your due date is February 12, which means you got pregnant in May." I started smiling. It happened when she came home from school and right after the dumb bitch aunt, attacked her.

"February 12th, huh."

"Yup. You may have a Valentines baby, if the baby wants to be stubborn and stay in."

"Damn, ma. I can't believe you're giving me a baby."

"Are you ok, with me keeping it? I don't wanna intrude on your life and.-" The doctor looked at me and I asked for privacy. She closed the door.

"Rak, there's not a woman in this world, I'd want to have my kids besides you. I'm sorry for always jumping to conclusions and I promise to listen first." She started crying.

89

"Marco, I don't know what I'm doing with this love thing and I keep running away because I think, you're gonna get fed up and leave me. I'm not experienced as you, in the bedroom, or anything else for that matter. All I know, is school. I promise to work harder at not running and talking to you. Please don't leave me." I wiped her eyes.

"One thing you don't have to worry about, is me leaving you. It's never gonna happen. I do appreciate you laying it out on the line, as far as you being scared. It means, I'm gonna have to work harder at showing you, how in love with you, I really am. I love you ma." I kissed her and she wrapped her other arm around me and slid her tongue in my mouth. We heard a knock at the door.

"Ms. Winters, I'm going to discharge you now. I'm sending you home with a prescription for pre-natal vitamins and a list of GYN doctors. You will have to follow up with one of them. Also, here's the card to another doctor, who will remove your stitches in a couple of weeks. Do you have any questions?"

"Can I still eat fast food?" I busted out laughing. Rak, had a banging ass figure but she loved fast food and greasy shit. I don't know how she kept the weight off and I wasn't complaining.

"Absolutely. Just try not eat it, everyday. You're going to gain weight and too much salty foods, can make your ankles swell." She handed me the paperwork.

"You ready."

"I don't wanna wear this shirt out. It has blood all over it." I went to take my shirt off and she yelled.

"NO!"

"What?"

"None of these women need to see your body. It's bad enough, they stared when we came in." I smirked. I saw them but I wouldn't tell her. It looks like she noticed anyway. I sent a text to Tech and told him, we were ready. He said, he'd be here shortly.

"Fine. Walk out in this gown. We can toss it, when we get home."

"Ok."

"You need anything before I go?" I asked when we got on the elevator.

"Cara, broke my laptop. All my work was on it and I don't know how I'm gonna get another one. Apple is very expensive and.-" I shushed her with a kiss.

"Don't insult me. Here." I took my black card out my wallet and handed it to her.

"No. I don't want your money." She pushed it back.

"I'll use the money in the account, my grandmother set up. I was saving it for when I get my own place, to buy furniture."

"Cancel that. You're moving in with me and if you wanna redecorate, be my guest. There's no more living with other people, when you have a man. Ma, let me give you what I know you deserve."

"What money?"

"No, the world." I lifted her face.

"There's nothing too expensive for me, or you. If you want it, you got it." She smiled.

"Oh, you have a new truck in the garage." I told her and helped her get in, when Tech pulled up.

"How you feel Rak?"

"It hurts to move my arm and neck. Hopefully, it will go away, since I can't take anything."

"Yup. We don't need my niece or nephew getting high in your stomach." She laughed and laid on my shoulder.

Once we got to the house, I helped her out. She wanted to take a shower before I left. She made me get a garbage bag, to cover the arm. After she finished, I helped her put on pajamas and get in the bed. I could tell she was tired and relieved at the same time.

"My card is on the dresser."

"Marco."

"Order the laptop and have it delivered for the next day. Get whatever you need with it and order anything else you want. There's no limit. All I ask, is you don't order another truck."

"I wouldn't."

"I'm just fucking with you. Sleep tight and call me if you need me."

"With what?" I pointed to the house phone and her cell. When Tech dropped us off, he went to Rahmel's and grabbed her books, phone and purse.

"Be careful, wherever you're going."

"Always." I kissed her and headed out the door.

"Marco!"

"Yea."

"I love you and thank you for always saving me."

"I love you too and trust me when I say; you're worth saving." She smiled. I left the bedroom door open and went downstairs.

"You ready to ride out?"

"Yup. Let's hit this nigga where it hurts." I set the alarm and closed the doors. When we got to the gate, I closed them and made sure the alarm was on it too. No one was gonna hurt her again and I mean that shit.

****

"Who is it?" A lady asked through the door.

"I'm here for Dennis."

"My son passed away. Who are you?"

"I know ma'am but I went to high school with him and I was in the neighborhood." Don't ask me why Tech, didn't let me kick the door in. Talking about he always wanted to do this. He started to ask for brown sugar, like Martin did in Bad Boys. We heard her unlock the door. I pushed it opened and put the gun, straight to her dome.

"Where is Z?" Her eyes grew wide. Tech shut the door behind us, while two of the guys we came with, searched the house.

"Marco, you already killed Dennis, why would you want Zaire too?" I forgot Dennis had a younger brother, when we were friends because he stayed out here in Connecticut. Once we found out, Z and Zaire, were the same, it all came together. He was fucking with Rakia, to get me. It probably wasn't intentional at first but once he saw us at the club; in my eyes, he made it his mission to fuck with her. Unfortunately, she had no idea.

"Dennis was a bitch ass nigga, who tried to take me out and lost his life. Zaire should've told you that, instead of making up that fake ass story, he died for no reason." I could see shock on her face. She always did believe anything they told her. Shit, Dennis told her, Mia was his girl first and I stole her from him so he stole her back. I know, the shit doesn't make no sense but she believed him; even though she saw me with Mia, a lot, since he was my best friend.

"Zaire, kidnapped my girl and did some foul shit to her, looking for me."

"No, he wouldn't hurt a woman."

"Try again. He's foul as fuck. Now, where the fuck is he?"

"I...I...I... don't know. He was here earlier and I haven't seen him since."

"I hope you said goodbye."

PHEW! PHEW! Her body dropped. I stepped over it and went to where the guys were.

"Yo, he was on some crazy shit." Tech said, when we looked around. This nigga had newspaper clippings of his brothers' murder, old photos of us together and mad guns. We continued searching the room and found a laptop. I opened it up and his email account was open. He must've forgot to turn it off before he left.

"What's that?" Tech asked.

"No clue." I clicked on it and instantly got mad. There was the video he sent me of Rak and him, fucking.

"Yo." Tech stood up and moved away. As crazy as it sounds, I started watching it.

The night he sent it to me, I saw him fucking her, shut it off and deleted it. Something told me to watch the entire thing this time and see, if I could figure out what Rak was talking about. I had to laugh because this nigga was done in less than three minutes and she didn't enjoy it at all. He had the nerve to fall on the side, like he had a workout. Shit, it takes me longer to eat her pussy.

I continued watching and it looked like they were arguing. The sound was very low on his computer but once I turned it up, I already knew, what was about to happen. You heard her say, she's never done it and she's not going to. I watched with hate in my eyes as he basically raped her mouth, came in it and told her to leave. I called Tech, in to make sure we saw the same thing.

"Man, I'm not watching her fuck him."

"You know, I wouldn't let you see my girls' pussy or any other part of her body. I want you to look at this and tell me what you think." He sat next to me and his face turned up.

"He may not have forcefully fucked her but he definitely, forced her to suck his dick. She's crying and everything. Did she just vomit?" I ran my hand down my face.

"I'ma need to find this nigga, ASAP. He's gonna wish he never fucked with her."

"Did he send that to anyone?" His question made me look in his sent inbox.

"Yo, he sent this shit out to over 50 people." I only know that because it says the first few names, on who you put in the mail and then the exact total.

"Call up our boy and have him log into this computer. I want him running a virus on every person's computer, he sent this to. I don't care if people saw it already. They won't be able to send it to anyone else."

Tech made the phone call and we sat there, waiting for the guy to log into the account. That's the good thing about knowing people who worked for Apple. They could get into anyone's computer, if it was from the company. He sent a virus to every email and the computers, it was sent to. He said, if anyone else opened it because it was forwarded, they would have a virus too. I told him, to check the internet on his computer to make sure, he didn't upload it to world star, or those other social media sites. The only porn video Rakia is making, will be with me.

"Let's get outta here." Doc poured gasoline all through the house. I grabbed a paper towel, set it on fire and dropped it on the floor. This entire place is gonna burn, with his mother and everything else in it. He's gonna learn, he fucked with the wrong nigga's woman.

Zaire (Z)

"Shit, keep sucking it." I pumped in and outta this chicks mouth. I'd been fucking her for the last two years. She did stop for a minute, when she caught the same shit, Rakia told me, I gave her. We both ended up, going down to the clinic and got treated.

"I'm cumming." She sucked me dry and I fell back on the bed. I loved the way, she handled me. No one could compare to what she did for me.

"You still with the weird bitch?"

"Don't talk about her like that?" She sat up.

"Let me find out you really like her."

"And if I did, why does it matter to you?"

"It doesn't, however, she must not be keeping you happy, if you're here."

"Whatever." I picked up my phone that was going off. I was unsure of the number but answered it anyway.

"Hello."

"Yo, where you at?" I looked at the number again and the voice, was unfamiliar. I didn't understand why someone was asking where I was.

"Who this?" He laughed in the phone.

"Your worst fucking nightmare."

"Who this?" I stood up and felt the chick rubbing on my dick, to get hard again. I slapped her hand away.

"When's the last time you saw your mother?"

"This morning. Yo, who this?"

"Bro, you should turn on the news." The person hung up.

"Turn the TV on."

"We're reporting live from Arsonia Street, where a fire broke out, about an hour ago and the firefighters, have been trying to get it under control. We've been told, a woman lives here with her son but no one knows, if either of them are home. We'll bring you more when we have it." I fell back on the bed.

The scene behind the reporter was horrific. The house was damn near burned to the ground. The only person, I could think of to do this, is Marco but he lives in Jersey. Why would

101

he come way up here, unless Rakia told him something? I felt

my phone vibrating again and it's the same number, that called

a few minutes ago.

"Where's my mother?" I didn't even say hello.

"You don't think she made it?" He was being funny.

"Look, nigga. You fucked around and kidnapped the

wrong niggas woman. Then you forced your dick in her mouth

and made her vomit. To make matters worse, you lied to your

mom about the death of your brother. It's all good though.

Your time is coming and very soon. I'll be in touch."

"FUCKKKKKKK!" I shouted and started getting

dressed. Why did I even think to go to war with him? Dennis

had me thinking he was weak, regardless; of what the streets

said. I left the chick sitting there looking crazy. She probably

wanted to ask questions but I never gave her the chance. I

picked my phone up and called Rakia.

"Hello." She sounded asleep.

"BITCH, you told Marco, what I did to you?"

"Zaire, why are you cursing at me and I didn't tell

anyone. I'm embarrassed it even happened. Why are you

calling me this late for nonsense?" I've never known her to lie and I can't say she is now but if she didn't tell him, how did he know? Then it dawned on me, that I sent the video. However, he would've known a lot sooner. He must've saw it on my computer. How could I be so stupid? I'm mad because I should've never moved in with my mother, when Dennis died. She too, was on my back about getting him, yet; I'm the one, who's doing all the work.

"The motherfucker is up here, killing peoples' mom and burning houses down."

"Marco, wouldn't do that Zaire."

"What the fuck is wrong with you? Are you retarded or slow? Bitch, I just said he was here." I sped in and outta traffic, tryna get to my mother's house. I heard the beeps in my ear, informing me, she hung up. I called her back.

"What Zaire?"

"Call your nigga up and tell him, to back off, or I'm gonna kill you."

"Zaire, why would you say that? I never did anything to you." I felt bad for putting her in the middle but he put my mother in it. I planned on leaving Rakia alone and only going after him but its war now.

"I'm gonna enjoy taking your life, in front of him." She hung up again and this time, I didn't call back.

I grabbed the hoodie I run with in the mornings, threw it on, put the hood up and walked down the street, to where my mom lived. I parked my car a few blocks over, in case, those niggas waited for me to show up and luckily, I did. Marco and Tech, were standing in front of a truck with a couple other dudes, smoking and talking. They bold as hell but I got something for their ass. I pulled my gun out and this stupid ass lady, screamed.

"DO IT!" Marco shouted and came walking towards me. This nigga is crazy. I let one shot off and missed.

"You ain't no street nigga, which is why you missed. I am though." He pulled his weapon out and I took off running.

"Keep running nigga, you won't get far." People started running and thank goodness, they did. He wasn't able to get me, with everyone in the way. I looked down and noticed he shot me in the leg but I refused to stop. Some woman was

104

going in her house, so I bum rushed my way in. I pulled my gun out and told her, she better not scream.

"Close the door. I'm not tryna kill you." She did like I said and mentioned she was a nurse. How ironic is this? She grabbed some things and started working on me. I passed out when I felt her, digging the bullet out.

****

"Where the fuck am I?" I sat up and saw some lady asleep on the chair. I forgot she helped me. I limped to the window and looked outside. Those niggas were still out there. Who the fuck are they waiting for? Do they sleep?

"Where you at?" I called Mary up.

"Home."

"I need you to come get me."

"What's the address and you owe me."

"What?"

"Man, I know all about the bounty on your head. My brother told me." I forgot he was in the streets.

"Supposedly, they know you're on some street and waiting for you to come out. You're gonna have to slip out and come over to New Britain. It's always crowded on that street, so they won't see you."

"How long?"

"Give me twenty minutes." I went through the back and through the neighbor's yard. She said twenty and its probably going to take me that long to get there, with my fucked-up leg. I made it down the street with my hoodie on. Every car riding by, had me paranoid as hell. I finally made it to New Britain and Mary, was just pulling up.

"Where to?"

"I don't even know. I can't go home, or to school. Can I stay with you?" She sucked her teeth.

"How did your corny ass, get caught up with men like them?" I explained everything to her and she shook her head, in disappointment.

"You go to law school, Zaire. Your future is set. Why would you try and avenge your brother's death? Those are street niggas, who got this whole state and others on lock. Do you know my brother told me, there's a 100k bounty on your head? He said, it's probably gonna go up, each day until they find you." I put my head back.

"Did you really rape and kidnap his girl?"

"It wasn't like that." I tried to show her the video but forgot my phone in my car. I told her what happened.

"You're a dead man walking. Look, you can stay for a few days but you have to go after that. I can't have them tearing my shit up, looking for you."

"Really!"

"Nigga, you lucky, I'm giving you a few days. After what you just told me, I should kick your ass out, or take you back to them. I can't believe, you would do some shit like that." She said and stayed quiet for the rest of the ride. I got out the car and went in the house. All I wanted to do was lie down and calculate my next move. I called my cousin up and told her, I'd be there in a few days. She's the only other person, I have. Plus, I know she hates Tech's wife. The two of us working together, will for sure, get those niggas.

Rakia

"Wake up, honey." I heard and turned over, to see Marco's mom, Elizabeth, who told me to call her Lizzie, standing there smiling and holding the phone. She came in late last night and tried to talk but I had to ask her if we could do it tomorrow. I guess, she's ready.

"I'm tired."

"I know but Marco, is on the phone. She passed it to me and walked out the room. I sat up and yawned, before saying hello.

"Hey ma. Did you sleep well?"

"Yea, did you?" I should've told him about Zaire but I'll wait until he gets home. Now, that he has me in his house, I'm not too worried about him finding me.

"I haven't slept yet. Where I'm at, required me to stay up all night. Listen, my mom is going to take you shopping, for clothes and whatever else you need."

"Marco, I haven't gotten up yet,"

"It's after eleven, Rak. If you wanna sleep all day, when I get there, you can."

"Fine!" I tossed the covers over my legs and stood up.

"Are you acting like a brat?" I pouted my lips out, knowing he couldn't see me.

"No." He laughed.

"Do me a favor Rak?"

"Ok."

"Lock the door and then face time me back, when you're about to get in the shower."

"Ugh, ok." I hung the phone up and used the bathroom before calling him. I started the shower and waited for him to answer.

"Put the phone on the shelf in the shower and get in."

"Huh?" He started laughing.

"I wanna watch you."

"Ummm."

"Stop being nervous, ma. It's just me and you know, I'm not about to let anyone see what you got." I was nervous at first but did it.

"Put some soap on the rag and lather it, all over your body." I did what he asked and I could hear him, saying damn.

"Wet your hair." My head went under the shower head.

"Lift your leg on the bench and massage your clit."

"Marco."

"Come on ma. I miss you and this is all, I get until, I get home." I smiled and did what he asked.

"Pretend, it's me, sucking on it." I closed my eyes and bit down on my lip. I've pleasured myself a lot but never with a man on the phone, or even in my presence.

"Shit, you look so fucking sexy." He continued talking and I noticed, he had his dick in his hand.

"I need you Marcoooooo. Oh my God, I'm gonna cum."

"Cum for me baby. I wanna see it." I rubbed faster and heard him moaning louder. My body released its juices and I could hear him saying, he did the same. I raised my fingers and put them to my lips.

"You should be tasting this."

"Hell yea, I should. Thank you Rak."

"For?"

"I know, you went out your comfort zone to accommodate me and trust, I'm gonna make it up to you. Fuck, I can't wait to see you."

"Anything else, you need from me?" I had my index finger in my mouth.

"You play too much." He smiled and told me to finish washing up and he'd see me soon.

****

"Is that all you need from the Apple store?" His mom asked. I purchased a new laptop, a case for it, a keyboard cover and an IPad. I was going to get a desktop to keep in the extra room. He told me to get it and use it for doing my schoolwork, so I didn't always have to use my laptop but I thought it would be too much.

"Yes. I'm going to wait and get the desktop later."

"No, you're not. We're getting it now."

"But, I don't have the desk, or any furniture in the extra room to put it on."

"Minor things, honey." She walked to the salesperson and requested a brand-new desktop. I tried to talk her out of it. Her ass, was determined to get it and told me to leave her alone. After it was paid for, she had the guard take all of it, to the car so we could do more shopping. I was weary because that was over four thousand dollars already, in one place.

She dragged me in the Louis Vuitton store, where I fell in love with a few purses, a book bag and some slippers. I picked up a belt, some glasses and a wallet for Marco. We went into Neiman Marcus, Prada, Gucci and so many other stores. I had to take a break to eat, because I was starving.

We walked into Joe's American Bar & Grill. I desperately wanted a cheeseburger and fries, with a strawberry-banana smoothie. We sat down and as we waited, I saw his mom turn her face up. I turned around and a woman was coming towards us. Lizzie stood up and tried to get to her first.

"Hello, ma." She said and I heard a loud ass smack. Everyone in the store turned around. The chick didn't react and stared at me.

"Why the fuck are you here?"

"This must be the new girlfriend." She walked over to me and this woman, was beyond gorgeous. Her body was amazing and whoever did her makeup, had to be a professional. She reminded me of a younger Jennifer Lopez.

"Mia, what do you want?"

"Besides, my man back, not much."

"Bitch, he hasn't seen you in years. Did you forget what you did to him?" I couldn't believe how rude Marco's mom was being to her.

"Doesn't matter. When I saw him the other day, he wouldn't look at me and we both know why." The lady brought my food out and I couldn't wait to eat. I picked up a fry and placed it in my mouth, as the two of them, went back and forth.

"And why is that?" His mom folded her arms.

"Because, one look at me and his feelings will resurface. Marco, never really got over me, so stop pretending. Plus, I know, this young, special needs looking chick, ain't doing shit for him." I sat there speechless. Why did she think I was special? Do I look it?

"Just go, Mia."

"What? You don't want her to know, I was his first love." She looked at me.

"Four years of his life and heart belonged to me, hun. Don't get comfortable because I'm here for him, and I will go to great lengths to make sure, he remembers why he fell in love with me. You'll be a distant memory, soon enough. Enjoy the dick while you can." She laughed the entire way out the place. I picked my burger up and finished eating. I didn't want Lizzie to know, how upset, the chick made me. Unfortunately, everything she said was on my mind.

For the rest of the day, I barely spoke and watched as she shopped. Each store, she tried to get me to purchase more. I told her, enough money was spent on me. Of course, she said not to let Mia, get to me because Marco, left her for a reason and never looked back. Its easy for her to say. She's not in love with a man, who has different chicks trying to kill her, for being with him.

I love Marco, with everything I have but this is getting ridiculous. I mean, is he even worth all the shit, I've encountered, since he's been in my life? I sent Ang, a text and asked her, if I could come over. She told me, not to ever ask to stop by. I had the guard drop me off there and his mom went to the house, to bring the stuff.

I knocked on the door and took Antoine from her. He was such a happy baby and I enjoyed every moment spent with him. We walked in the kitchen and she was cooking lasagna. I know, my fat ass ate not too long ago; however, my stomach was growling like crazy. I sat in the chair, as she layered the pan and talked about her and Tech, working on another baby. I guess, me not responding caused her to stop and look at me. She placed the pan in the oven, washed her hands and sat next to me at the table.

"What happened?" I explained everything the chick said and she agreed, that his baggage was becoming too much. She also said, I can't run and need to discuss my feelings about it, with him. Give him the chance to fix it.

"I don't know, Ang. I'm not trying to run and I'm being an adult, when I say this." I wiped my eyes.

"I love him and he loves me. Unfortunately, is it enough for me to accept the baggage, abuse and violence, I've encountered, since he and I, have been together? I get running away isn't the answer. But, I'm thinking of, how much more can I take? I have a baby to protect now and worrying about being attacked and threatened, each time, I step out the house, is crazy. So again, I ask. Is he worth it?" She took my hand in hers.

"Only you an answer that question, Rak." She smiled.

"What?"

"I am already starting to see growth in you and I'm proud."

"Because I asked, is he worth it?"

"No, because you're putting yourself first. You want his love but you don't wanna fight for it and shouldn't have to. Rak, we all know relationships are hard and you're constantly working at it but do what you need to, for yourself and the baby."

"I don't want him to be with another woman but I can't use that as an excuse, not to leave. Ang, I thought Bobbi and Cara, were pretty but this woman is fucking gorgeous. I'm not saying, I'm ugly but she was his first love and regardless of whatever they went through, it doesn't change the fact, she's confident in getting him."

"I'm not gonna argue with anything you said. Rak, I can't imagine what you're going through and like I said before, you are the only one who needs to make the decision to leave or stay. I will support any decision you choose. I can't say he will but I got your back. Me and Antoine. Right lil man." She took him off my lap and he giggled.

The two of us ate dinner together and even watched a few movies before going to bed. I decided to stay the night because I really needed to make a decision. She gave me a brand-new pair of leggings and a shirt, to wear for bed and I placed all my clothes in the washer. I needed clean panties in the morning. After, putting them it the dryer, I went to the spare room and laid on the bed.

Marco, had called me again for the hundredth time. I'm sure his mom told him everything because he kept asking me, to pick up. In another text he said, she'll never be in his life again and I wanted to believe him but it was so hard, when she was confident and they had history. I may be slow, but I'm not that slow. Everyone knows, its hard to get over your first love. Shit, he's mine and I can't even fathom trying to get over him, so I know what she's talking about. I refused to answer and sent a text.

Me: *Marco, I'm not running or angry at you, so please don't assume that. I'm trying to wrap my head around all the things, I've encountered since we've been together. I love you so much and I've been attacked, verbally, and physically because of the love, I have for you. I have to ask myself, if it's worth it. In my heart, I know you are, trust me, I do. But our baby doesn't deserve to be stressed out in my belly, because his or her mom is. I don't want to lose it and I'm afraid the drama in your life, is going to do just that. I hope you understand and give me the time, I need to figure things out. I love you."* I hit send and waited for him to respond.

Marco: *Bet!* Is the only response, I received? Is he upset with me? Maybe, I should've called him. No, be a grown-up Rakia and figure things out on your own. He has to respect your choice. I kept telling myself until, I fell asleep. I sure hope, I'm doing the right thing.

Mia

I wanted to punch Marco's mom in the face; however, I know he'd probably kill me. Who the hell did she think she was, putting her hands on me and in front of his new whore. Yea, Bobbi told me about her slow ass. She told me the girl Cara, she was currently sleeping with, claimed she was retarded. A man like. Marco, had no business with a woman, who couldn't handle him. I mean, was he doing an experiment or something? Why was he settling for fish and grits, when he could have steak and potatoes?

I admit, she was beautiful and I could see why he became attracted to her. She had an innocent look, you could tell her hair was natural and Marco, loved a woman with her own hair. He always said, he ain't want shit falling in his hands, when he was yanking it, while fucking. Just thinking about how well, he used to handle my body, made me fantasize for a brief moment.

Unfortunately, Dennis and I, ended up sleeping together behind his back. It happened by accident but we never stopped. I'm not going into a long drawn out story on it. Just know, we were at a party, and Marco wasn't there. Dennis came to get me for him and on the way home, I was horny and decided to give him head. Instead of stopping me, he allowed me to continue. He pulled over on the side of the road and we had sex. It was good but Marco was better. The affair continued for the next few months and neither of us planned on falling for each other, or him finding out.

To be honest, I was happy he did. The hiding and sneaking around was becoming too much. I saw all the hurt on Marco's face when he witnessed us, the night of prom. It was then, I knew, he was the right one for me. Don't ask me why, I just knew. By then, it was too late and the secret was out, about my pregnancy too. Dennis and I, went to school the following Monday and told everyone, we were a couple. People talked about us like a dog. Wondering how his best friend could do him like that and said his so-called girlfriend, was a ho.

Tech tried to kill Dennis, while Marco, kept his head held high, like nothing bothered him. I respected him so much more, for not entertaining everyone else. Of course, the bitches began to throw themselves at him and I was pissed. It didn't take long for them to say he was fucking everything in sight. I was devastated to know other women, now had, what I had. I tried to talk to him countless times but he would ignore me and walk past, as if I didn't exist.

After graduation, I ran into him and he was disgusted, when he noticed my stomach. He knew about the pregnancy but I guess, seeing it was different. He and I, spoke on children all the time but he wasn't ready, which is why he always strapped up and checked the condom, when we finished. He wanted to have time for his family and he knew it would take a few years to get where he wanted to be. Yea, he was a hustla and already had money but he wanted to be on top.

Eventually, he did it and now he's the most sought out man from kingpins, dealers and women. I know all about Bobbi, sleeping with him for the last few years because she blasted photos of them all over social media. I befriended her a year ago because now that Dennis was deceased, my money was low. I really wanted to live wealthier and the only person who could accommodate me, is Marco.

Yes, I still love him and never should've cheated but at the time, I was young and trying to have fun. Shit, we were together for four years and we were always around each other. I even hung on the block, with him sometimes. I've never known Marco to cheat and I always wanted to be near him. I loved Dennis but never the way, I loved Marco. However, I knew once he found out about us, we could never be again. Now, I'm here to reclaim what's mine and start the family, we planned a long time ago.

I stepped on the porch of the new condo, I purchased and felt a piece of steel on the back of my head. No one knew, I was in town so who the hell is here? I tried to turn around to see who it was but he wouldn't let me. It no longer mattered because I smelled his cologne. He wore the same kind, that day at Bobbi's. I unlocked the door and he pushed me in. I had to use my arms to stop me from falling flat on my face. I stood up and turned around to see Marco standing there, with an aggravated look on his face.

"Hey baby." He smirked and yoked my ass right up.

"If you ever say anything else to my girl, I'm gonna do to you, what I should've done a long time ago."

"You're putting hands on me, for her?"

"You had no fucking right to approach my mother, or spit those bullshit ass lies to Rakia. Then you call her names. You don't even know her."

"Marco, please let go." His eyes softened up and he released my shirt.

"Stay the fuck away from her." He went to the door.

"So that's it. You don't love me anymore?"

"Nah, Mia. What you did, can never be forgiven. As far as love, I'll always have love for you because you were my first. But you'll never get my heart again and that's some real shit." He put his hand on the door and I ran over there.

"Move, Mia." I slid under his arm and made him face me. He turned his head and I used my hand to make him.

"I messed up Marco."

"I don't wanna hear that."

"We were young Marco."

"So, the fuck what Mia. I could've had mad bitches but I didn't." He moved away from the door and sat on the couch.

"I'm sorry." I let the tears fall. I really did love him and wanted to love him again. Not just for the money but to show him, I'm serious.

"Mia, it took me a very long time, to love another woman. I'm not trying to lose her." He sat there with his arms on his knees.

"Are you in love with her?"

"Very much so. She's gonna be my wife." He said it without flinching.

"I thought you said, you'd never marry anyone but me." I stood in front of him and lifted his face.

"That was before Mia. If we broke up and you were with another nigga and came back, I'd be ok, with taking you back. But that was my boy, my partner, he was like, my other brother. What were you thinking?" He laid back on the couch and I moved on his lap.

"I wasn't Marco and I'm so sorry for hurting you." And just like that, we were engaged in an aggressive, yet, passionate kiss. I knew he still loved me and this only proved it.

I removed my shirt, and bra and his mouth found my breasts. He sucked on them gently and caressed them, in a way, only he knew how. I stood up, removed the rest of my clothes and watched him lick his lips. I wasted no time, getting on my knees and pleasing him. He was pumping in and out my mouth and I enjoyed, taking all of him in. I placed one hand under his balls and felt his body stiffening up.

"Ahhhh." He spit all he had in my mouth and I swallowed, every last drop. Say what you want but I'm getting my man back. I walked in the room and grabbed some condoms. Yup, I knew he'd come around after hearing what I said to his girl. I also knew, he wouldn't trust me in the beginning which is why, I never opened the package. He blew his breath out and took them from me. He never said a word, slid the condom on and fucked me silly. I remember him being good but his stroke game, was outstanding and after going most of the night, I wanted more. He refused without protection, so a bitch got dressed, went to the store and picked up more.

"Mia. I shouldn't be here." He said. I kissed down his chest and placed him in my mouth. He ignored his conscience and gave me what I wanted, three more times. We literally didn't stop until, the next afternoon. His phone went off so many times, he ended up turning it off. I didn't give a fuck. I snuggled up under him and fell asleep in his arms, just like old times. I finally had my man back and no one, is going to keep me away.

****

BOOM! BOOM! BOOM! BOOM! I heard someone banging on my door. I looked up and Marco was still knocked out. The clock on my phone read, ten at night. We must've slept the entire day away.

BOOM! BOOM! BOOM! BOOM! The banging continued. I threw my robe on, shut the bedroom door and went to see who it was. I opened it and was shocked to see him. He moved past me and went straight to my bedroom.

"Tech, what are you doing?"

"Don't say shit to me, bitch. You knew exactly, what the fuck you were doing."

"What?" He ignored me and went in my room.

"Marco, get up." I could tell he was out of it still. Tech, told him to get up again.

"Shit, what you doing here? What time is it?"

"Nigga, I've been calling you all night and day. Here it is the next night and you still laid up with this ho."

"Come on Tech, don't call her that."

"WHAT?" I was shocked he defended me and I think Tech, was too.

"I'm saying, she didn't make me come or stay here."

"Righttttt. Well, why you were laid up on your own, Rak has been to the hospital for stress and high blood pressure."

"Say what?" He started rushing to get dressed and Tech, walked out the room.

"What happened to her?"

"Look Marco. Maybe its best you stay away from her for a few days." I stood there listening to them.

"Why would you say that?"

"One… you have a bunch of hickeys on your neck. Two… you stayed here all night. She worried herself to death because she wanted to talk to you and your phone was off. And last but not least, it looks like you have some unfinished business here. What the fuck were you thinking, sleeping with her." He gave me a disgusting look.

"Tech, my business, is my business." That surprised me. The two of them never disagreed on anything. Tech, nodded and was on his way out.

"You right. Do me a favor though?" He turned around.

"When you're out doing your business, let Rak know, so she isn't crying half the night, worrying that someone killed or hurt you. Let her know, you're fine and fucking the next bitch."

"Tech."

"Nah, she has my wife stressing out and that shit don't sit right with me." *His wife?* I didn't even know he was married.

"I'm out." He looked me up and down, with a snarl on his face and slammed the door. Marco, fell on the couch. I could see how torn he was but it worked out for me. His chick was mad and I got the dick. Who could ask for anything more?

Tech

Trying to figure out this nigga and why he fucked with the bitch, who broke his heart and fucked his best friend, is the least of my worries. Unfortunately, I had to find him because Rak, ended up in the hospital. The doctor said she was stressed out so bad, it caused a spike in her blood pressure. She didn't need any medication but was told to take it easy, or she could possibly lose the baby. Ang, had me sitting there, damn near all day. I was going to leave sooner but then she'd get mad.

Once the doctor gave Rak the discharge papers, I dropped her and Ang, off at the house. She asked where I was going and I said, to find Marco. I knew exactly where he was, because he mentioned going over Mia's and threatening her, to stay away from Rak. I asked if he wanted me to come and he said no. He would only be a minute and was coming to speak with Rak, at my house. Well, that was yesterday afternoon and here we are the next night and his ass was over there knocked the fuck out. I'm not judging him for doing his thing but when

I have to lie to my wife about where he is because she's best friends, with his woman, it's a problem for me.

If that's not an issue, I still had to try and find out who sent this dude, to run my wife off the road. He was trying to kill her and I had no clue, who would want to hurt her. It couldn't be Zaire because I don't think Rak, ever mentioned Ang and even if she did, he wouldn't know who she was. Again, it leaves me in the dark and it bothered me. Ang, went out with my son and someone still managed to get her. The crazy part is, no one bothers her, when we're out together. Should I assume, the person doesn't want me dead? All I know, is I need to find out who this person is and fast.

I walked in the house, locked the door and found my wife and her best friend in the living room, on opposite couches; asleep. I picked Ang up and made our way up the steps. She woke right up when I laid her on the bed. I started undressing and walked in the bathroom to shower. I had a long day and this hot water would definitely, relax me.

"Did you find him?" She asked and stepped in with me.

"Yea. I don't wanna talk about it, right now." She nodded. That's what I loved about her. If I said, I didn't wanna talk, she'd give me my space until I was ready.

"I love you Ang and I promise not to ever hurt you again." She gave me a weird look. I messed up once and she took me back. I can't imagine her giving me another chance, if I did it again.

"I know and you don't have to keep saying it. I believe you." She stood on her tippy toes to kiss me. My arms lifted her up and she happily slid down.

"Sssssss. You feel so good Antoine." She bit on my neck and dug her nails in my back.

"How good?"

"Real good." Our tongues met. I leaned her against the wall and gave her pussy a beating. I wasn't angry. I just needed a nut and the only one who could give it to me, is her.

After we finished and got in the bed, there was a light knock at the door. We both knew it was Rak, because my son is still a baby and no one else is here. I threw a t-shirt on and sat up in the bed. I didn't think it was appropriate to be laid up in the bed damn near naked and she come in. Ang, asked her if she were ok and she looked at me.

"Is he ok? Did you find him?" I looked at Ang. She had no idea either.

"Yea. He's good." Rak, is no dummy so the next question out her mouth didn't surprise me.

"He's with her, right?" I put my head down.

"Tech."

"Rak, don't ask a question you don't want the answer to."

"I knew it." She leaned against the wall.

"I didn't say yes."

"Tech, I've been around long enough to know, when you don't wanna tell something. Not that you're keeping secrets but you know what I'm saying. Don't worry, you didn't have to tell me because I felt it in my heart. I knew, once he didn't answer for me, she had him."

"Sis, are you ok?" Ang ran over to her.

"Yup, I will be." She wiped her eyes and stepped out the room.

"Rak." Ang went behind her and walked in the spare room.

"I'm ok, y'all." Ang looked at me with sad eyes. I couldn't control what the nigga did. Nor, did I want a part in the shit.

"Rakia, you can stay here for as long as you want." I told her and leaned on the door.

"Thanks, but no thanks. It's time for me to do grown up things."

"What?" Ang sat next to her.

"I have the money my grandmother saved up for me. I'm going to get an apartment, some cheap furniture, a hoopty and call it a day. It's time."

"I'll help you with whatever you need."

"It's ok."

"I'm not taking no for an answer." She looked at me and I nodded, to let her know, we had her for whatever.

"Tech, I know that's your brother but all I'm asking, is that you don't tell him anything about me."

"You're pregnant by him."

"I'll send him ultrasound photos and promise to call, when I'm in labor. Please Tech. I need you to do this." I ran my hand down my face. Ang, gave me a look saying, I better agree.

"Fine." I walked away and went to my room. She didn't want me to tell him, where she'd go and I know, for a fact, he doesn't want her to know where he is. They both had me in a fucked up situation. Ang, came in the room and climbed in the bed.

"I know, it's hard for you to be in this situation. But she's pregnant baby and the less stress, the better. If she continues, it's a possibility the baby won't make it, full term." I sat there quiet.

"It's gonna be fine Tech." She kissed me and laid on my chest.

"I hope so because being in the middle, sucks."

****

"I haven't seen you in a while." Shana said and sat next to me at the bar.

"Move around." Ang and I, were at the club, having drinks. Her parents had the baby and we wanted to have a night out and enjoy ourselves. We asked Rakia to join but she was too afraid of running into Marco. I knew for a fact, he wouldn't be here because he was caught up with Mia. I only know that because I rode by the house, when I ran out to take my son to Ang's parents and his car was there.

"Tech, why can't we be together?"

"Because he's married bitch." Ang lifted my hand up and showed my ring. Shana, clearly saw it and gave zero fucks.

"You still salty about me sucking his dick?" Ang laughed and sat down.

"Never. He made me the wife. I own him."

"Do you?" She was trying hard to press my wife's buttons.

"Yes ma'am. You tried again and he wasn't beat, correct."

"Only because you're here."

"No, it's because he won't risk this." She pointed to my heart.

"He won't risk getting his hurt, or hurting mine. It's called being in love and not letting fake ass, side bitches destroy what we worked hard to build. Ain't that right baby?" She slid her tongue in my mouth and I sat her on my lap.

"Don't even stoop to her level. You know who I belong to."

"What the fuck ever. He'll be back." Ang waved her off and she left. If things couldn't get any worse, Marco walked in with Mia, close behind him. So much for him not showing up. I tried to keep my wife, from turning around but it was no use. He came straight to me and sent Mia, to find a table. I guess, he knew not to fuck with Ang.

"We got a problem."

"And you couldn't come speak about it, without your ho?" Ang, got up. I felt the same way. Since when did he start bringing bitches to speak to me? I could see if it were Rak. She was his baby mama and supposed to be, his wife.

"I'm not gonna disrespect you Ang and I know you're feeling some type of way, but it ain't what you think."

"So those hickeys aren't what I think? Thank goodness, Rakia didn't come. Do you know what that would've done to her, to see you two together?"

"I see it, Ang." We turned around and Rakia was standing there, trying her hardest not to cry.

"I came to get out the house but it looks like, I should've stayed in."

"Rak, can I talk to you?"

"HELL NO!" She screamed out, shocking all of us. His facial expression changed. I knew, it was time to separate him from her.

"Marco, you brought me here to spend time with this bitch?" Ang, snapped her neck and so did he.

"Aye! Tha fuck you say?" Mia got nervous.

"Nothing. I'm ready to go."

"Wait for me, over there, like I said. And don't bring your ass over here again." Like the lost puppy she is, Mia went to the table.

"Ang, this wasn't a good idea. I'll see you later."

"Rak."

139

"Marco, don't say shit to me, with those fucking hickeys on your neck. You didn't even have the decency, to cover them up." She walked out and he tried to chase her but I blocked him.

"Man, you know she can't drive when she's upset."

"Ang, go with her." I said and she ran out but not before mushing him in the head.

"I'ma fuck you up later, Ang." She stuck her middle finger up and kept walking. Those two stayed arguing, like brother and sister. That's why I never got in it. He would never disrespect my wife and I would never, do it to Rak. The other bitch Mia though. I'll play her the fuck out and won't think twice.

"Z, is in town." He picked up the beer he ordered and took a swig.

"Does anyone know where?"

"Nah. I've had someone staking out Shana's place but nothing, yet. How is she?" He took another sip.

"Who?"

"Don't play."

"Bro, you know I don't like to get in your shit but you put me in it. She's having your seed. How could you do her like that?"

"Honestly.-" He was about to speak and this bitch walked up.

"Marco, I'm ready. Hey Tech." I sucked my teeth.

"Why are you so angry? You act like, I fucked around on you." I laughed.

"Marco, get your girl." He wasn't gonna say anything because we both knew, he still wanted Rak. We may have disagreed in front of Mia, about them sleeping together but when it came to me speaking my mind, he never interrupted and vice versa.

"No, Marco. I wanna know why he has an attitude? You barged in my house and started calling me ho's." I didn't even allow her dumb ass to finish.

"It's what you are and whenever my brother is in your house, or anyone else's, you damn right, I'ma barge the fuck in." Marco had a smirk on his face. We never allowed a bitch to get in between us. Plus, his crazy ass would bust down a bitch door, if the roles were reversed.

"You didn't have to fuck me, for me not to like you. He may forgive you but I don't owe you shit. I'm out bro." I slammed my drink down and walked out before, my hands made it around her throat.

Rakia

"Do you prefer all hundreds, or it doesn't matter?" The bank teller asked, when I withdrew, 10k from my account.

"Hundreds are fine. It's easier for me to count." We started laughing. She handed me the envelope and I headed out to the car with Ang. She and I, had been out all day, picking up things for the small condo, I got at a good price. The day we went, the person met us there, liked me, took my check and told me, I could move in whenever. I got the keys and said, why not today?

"You ready?"

"As ready as, I'll ever be." She looked at me and smiled.

"I'm proud of you Rak."

"Why?"

"Because you're hurting and still handling business."

"I'm hurting but I have to do this. He made his choice Ang and it would be stupid of me, to stay in the house. If he wants to be with her, they can live there together. I damn sure won't be like some of these women, who share a house with the baby daddy and his chick."

"I wouldn't do it any differently."

"Do you think, I'm running?"

"Not this time. You're right about him moving on so why would you stay? Granted, he hasn't asked you to leave but who would stay?" She said when we pulled up at the house.

"Are you sure him and Tech, aren't here?" I asked and pressed the code to the gate.

"Yea. I asked Tech, to keep him away for at least an hour or two." I nodded and she pulled in. We stepped out and I took a deep breath. This house is everything and more to me. I'm going to miss it.

I pressed the alarm on the house, went in the kitchen to grab some bags and walked up the steps. I opened the door and broke down. The bed was still made and all the items, I purchased that day in the mall with his mom, were laid out everywhere. I went through each bag and only took out the things, I'd really need, like the laptop, its case and the IPad. I didn't really need the IPad but I wanted it. I removed one Louis Vuitton purse, one pair of the red bottoms and a pair of Jordan's. Everything else, remained in the bag.

I went to the dresser and only took out the things, I brought with me from my cousin's house. Rahmel, brought me a lot of things from Target, like pajamas, clothes and his girl picked me out the underclothes. I noticed the expensive lingerie set, Ang told me to buy, to wear for him, in the drawer the day we were at Short Hills mall. The same day, my aunt destroyed my truck and Zaire called himself, kidnapping me. He must've saved all the things that were in the other truck. But when did he put them in here? I don't recall seeing them before.

It didn't take me long to pack my things and I only left with two bags. One was the few items his mom and I, shopped for and the rest were the things, I brought with me. I walked in the bathroom, removed my toothbrush and hygiene products too. He didn't need to have any remnants of me left here. I'm sure his chick wouldn't appreciate seeing it anyway.

Ang, came in and asked if I were ready. I took the envelope of money out my pocket and placed it on the bed. People may think, I'm crazy for giving it to him. However, he didn't have to buy me, to stay with him. I'm not saying he was but the things I'm leaving with from the mall, the day I went shopping with his mom, came up to the exact total, I withdrew from the bank so I'm giving him, his money back.

"Yea, I'm ready." We walked down the steps. She opened the door and I took one more look at the house. I should destroy everything in here, like a ratchet chick would. But where would it get me? He still wouldn't be my man and my heart would still be broken. I set the alarm on the door, put my things in the car and made sure the gate closed too. I was depressed leaving his estate but its what's best and I knew it.

Ang, dropped me off at the small condo and helped me bring things in and put them away. We also blew up the air mattress to make sure no holes were in it, in case, we had to go back to the store. Ang and I, were going furniture shopping tomorrow because she wouldn't take no for an answer, about purchasing stuff. I left the subject alone and walked her downstairs, to her car.

"Remember the alarm company is coming early, so be up." Tech, paid extra so the people could come the following day. He didn't want me to move out as it was but he said, if I did, a security system had to be set up. I don't know why, when this area has mad old people. It was perfect too because it would be peaceful.

"After they're done, call me so we can pick out furniture."

"Ok." She hugged me.

"Love you sis." I waved, ran in the house and put both locks on the door.

I glanced around the house and it was pretty spacious for a two bedroom. I had so many ideas, for how I wanted to decorate. I looked on the floor and the television was still in the box. I pulled it out, along with the Blu-ray player and put in one of Kevin Hart's comedy specials. I needed to laugh and he could make it happen. I started putting the curtains up, making the bed, putting the rest of the groceries away and ended up falling asleep right after.

****

"Let me find out, you don't know me anymore." Ang came in with lil Antoine.

"I'm sorry." It's been two weeks and all I've been doing is sleeping and doing class work. If I wasn't doing that, I was working.

I found a job as an Entry Level, Electrical Engineer in Morristown, NJ. The pay was $16 an hour and had great benefits. I didn't need a job right now but the money I had saved, would run out eventually, so I did what I had to. The people were so nice there and the boss loved me already.

"You know, you can come over anytime you want." She waved me off.

"Soooooo, Marco's been asking about you." She plopped on the sofa. I picked out a nice living room set, when we went furniture shopping and I think she loved it, more than me. Her and Tech, spared no expense on my stuff. I mean, my bedroom set was a California King and we all know those are expensive. I've never slept in a bed so big, except Marco's. The dining room set was beautiful and the baby's room wasn't decorated yet, because I was superstitious. However, they promised to take me shopping when I was ready. Little did they know, that's something, I'm doing on my own.

"I don't care."

"Yea, ok. Anyway, he wants to see you."

"No, thank you." I had the baby on my lap.

"I don't blame you." She said and flipped through the channels.

"Oh, can you give him this, the next time you see him?" I handed her an envelope. She opened it and smiled.

"He's gonna love this." It was an ultrasound photo of the baby. I kept my end of the bargain, so Tech wouldn't tell where I was.

"Can you take me to the store?" I asked and she nodded yes.

"What's wrong with your car?" I did buy me a 2014 Nissan Rogue and it was in great shape. It only had 24,000 miles on it and one owner. You can't beat that. I didn't go out, besides to work anyway so I didn't need anything fancy.

"Nothing. I like riding in yours." She laughed. We piled in the car and was singing all the songs on the radio. Even lil man, was making noise in the back seat.

I grabbed all types of food, snacks, and whatever else, I thought was needed. It was only me but Rahmel stopped by a few times a week, with his girlfriend and had me cooking for them. She was so nice and I loved her, for him. He's been giving me money too. I ask him to stop, but he tells me, he won't because I'm alone and he never wants me to be without again. I loved my cousin and wished we were still roommates. However, this is what I needed to do. Who knew, living on your own could be fun, peaceful and sometimes lonely? I enjoyed it though. It won't be lonely for long, when my baby comes.

"Yea, Marco and I, are together again." I froze when someone said that. Did she just say they were a couple? I knew he was probably sleeping with others but a couple?

Unfortunately, when I saw who it was, I sucked my teeth. I wouldn't put it past her for trying to rub it in my face.

"Let's go Rak. I have my son." I understood because we didn't need anything popping off.

"Looky here." Ang and I, were placing things on the conveyor belt. I pushed the cart ahead of me, to make sure lil man, was blocked and she could move him, if this chick got crazy.

"Hello. Mia, is it?" I continued watching the lady ring me up.

"You know my name, bitch."

"WOW! I'm a bitch. You don't even know me."

"Stay away from Marco, or I'll beat your ass worse than its ever been."

"Not a problem. I haven't seen him in weeks. You're doing a great job occupying him." I gave her a thumbs up and helped the cashier bag the few items. It wasn't anything cold and mostly can and box foods for sides, to my meals.

"Keep it that way." Ang, pushed the cart.

"What do you want from me Mia, Huh? You came here to get Marco and you have him. Why are you bothering me?"

"Because I know it's you, he's been spending the night with." Shock had to be written on my face. She knew too because she rolled her eyes.

"I'm sorry to tell you this but we haven't spoken or seen one another, since I found out about you two. If he hasn't been with you, its someone else. Have a good night." I walked next to Ang and she kept looking behind, to make sure she didn't run up on me, as she says.

"Can you believe he's been with someone else?" Ang, never responded.

"Ang?" She looked at me and then the road.

"What?" I stared at her.

"He's not with anyone else."

"How do you know?"

"Tech, told me, he's been at some other house, he has. No one has really spoken to him."

"Oh."

"I didn't tell you because you said, you're done with him."

"Good." We rode the rest of the way in silence. I grabbed the few bags and told her, I'd call her later.

I locked up, put the alarm on and started a bath. It always relaxed me. I stepped in and laid back. It felt good to kick back and do nothing. Once I got out, there was a knock at my door. Ang, Tech and Rahmel are the only ones who knew about this place, so it had to be one of them. I threw my pajama pants on, the tank top, robe and went downstairs. I opened the door and got the shock of my life.

Marco

"Can I come in?" I asked Rak, when she opened the door. I could see how surprised she was that I was here.

"Umm, yea, I guess." She stepped aside and stood at the door.

"It looks nice in here." I surveyed the condo and smiled.

The night she saw me at the club with Mia, I knew she would leave me; which is why, I wouldn't even go to the mansion. I didn't wanna see all her things missing. Once Tech, told me she moved out, I gave him money to give her, to use for whatever she wanted. I don't care, if it was to build a house from the ground up. My motto has always been with her, *if she want it, she got it* and it won't change because I fucked up. She is still the mother of my child and will be my wife. Hell yea, I'm claiming it.

"Thanks. What are you doing here? Matter of fact, how did you know where I lived?" I took a seat on the couch.

"To be honest, I don't know why I'm here." She rolled her eyes and closed the door.

"I guess its because, I know, I hurt you real bad and wanted to check on you."

"Marco, Ang has the ultrasound picture for you." She ignored my comment.

"Sit, Rak." I patted the seat next to me.

"I'm fine standing. You won't be here long." I nodded my head.

"Let me start off by saying, I'm sorry for hurting you. I never meant to drag you in any of my nonsense. From day one, its been bullshit coming from the baggage in my life." She put her head down.

"No matter how many times, you tried to break free, you still came back to me but this time it's different and I know it. You won't talk to me, text or even let me see you. I'm surprised you even opened the door." She stood there silent.

"As far as, how I know where you live, I had to beg Tech to tell me. You know Ang wasn't giving you up. I give it to him though, he held out for a while. I guess, he got tired of me asking and broke." She shook her head with a slight grin on it. Tech, may be her friend but he's my brother. How long did she really expect him to hold out on me?

"Rak, I swear, my intentions were to go see her and tell her to leave you alone. I cursed her out and went to leave. Next thing I know, she's apologizing and on my lap, kissing me." I saw the tears falling down her face.

"I fucked up ma and I've been regretting it ever since." I stood up and walked over to her. She backed away and used her hand to keep me at a distance.

"You damn right, you fucked up." I stared at her.

"That night, I thought about the text, I sent and wanted to talk about it with you. If you could promise me she wasn't a factor, I planned on staying with you. Then, I called you all night, the next day and couldn't get an answer. My anxiety was through the roof because, I thought something happened to you. Ang and Tech, stayed with me at the hospital because my own man, couldn't be there for me. Do you know how that feels? Marco, I almost had a heart attack because I couldn't calm down and YOU WERE LAID UP WITH YOUR EX. THE

SAME EX, WHO HURT YOU, AS YOU SAY. THE SAME ONE, YOU HATED." Her head was on the wall and the tears were pouring down her face.

I wiped as much as I could because they wouldn't stop. I felt like shit hearing she could've died. However, she was right. How could I not answer for her? Why did I even risk what we had, for a woman who did me wrong? She put both of her hands on the side of my face and looked into my eyes.

"I never asked to love you, or to fall in love. You made me and baby, I was happy. And even through the violence I endured; in my eyes, you were so worth it. Nothing anyone could say to me, would make me leave you; except her and you know why." She walked away from me.

"Because in my heart, I knew you still loved her. She did something bad to you, and once you laid eyes on her, you forgave her and left me out in the cold. There was no Rakia, Bobbi or anyone else. Everything revolved around your first love and you know it." I couldn't dispute anything she said. The moment my eyes met Mia's, it was like, we were teenagers again. My feelings resurfaced and no one could get in between us.

"I'm not these other women Marco, who throw themselves at you, or allow you to treat them like shit. You said I was special and you'd never hurt me but you did. I didn't deserve any of this and yet, you instilled so much pain in my life and never gave a fuck."

"You are special to me and I do love you."

"Yea right." I pushed her against the wall, shocking myself. Never in my life, did I ever think, my hands would be on her.

"That's right. Get angry at what you did and take it out on me. It's what you do best." I removed my hands from her shirt.

"What do you want me to do, Rak? She was there before you and.-"

"You're right. I don't expect you to do anything but be Marco." She went to open the door.

"I wasn't grown up, enough for you. I couldn't give you what you needed sexually, mentally, or physically. If I could, or if your heart was truly with me, she would've never been able to bed you. We both know it." I hate when women say that shit. You can be madly in love with a woman and fall victim to pussy. A man, may have fucked up but it doesn't take his love away or mean, he didn't love her.

"FUCK!" I punched a hole in her wall and she jumped.

"Please go."

"Give me one more chance Rak."

"For you to do the same thing? It would be stupid of me, knowing she's here. I'd be setting myself up for failure and another heartbreak. I may be new to this love thing but I'm not crazy."

"Rak, I won't ever see her again. Just give me another chance. Please baby. I can't live without you."

"Marco, don't make this harder than it already is."

"I'm going to kill her tonight."

"WHAT?"

"If you need to be sure, I won't be with her again, in order to come home, I'll do it. Rak, I'm dying without you. Please don't leave me." She wiped the tears, now falling from my eyes. I was in love with this woman and she no longer wanted me. She walked over to the door.

"I can't risk it. Our baby, may not make it."

"Rak, close the door." She refused.

"Go home, Marco."

"FUCK THAT! It's not home, if you're not there."

"Please, just go." She was crying hysterically.

"I'm gonna win you back." I placed my hands on her face and kissed her lips.

"I promise, you're gonna be my wife." She closed the door behind me and I could hear her let out a loud scream and fall against the door. I thought about going back in but she was right. Mia, is a factor in my life and it wasn't right to bring Rak, in more of my shit. If it's the last thing, I do. She'll be my woman again.

****

"What Mia?" She had been calling me non-stop, since we slept together. We weren't a couple and I hadn't fucked her since the night, Tech came and got me. The only reason, she came with me to the club, is because she's the one, who

160

informed me of Z, being in town. He called and asked where she was because his mom passed away. Evidently, they were close and told her he was staying in Jersey.

"Why are you dodging me?"

"Mia, what we did was a mistake."

"Why? You know, I love you."

"Again. Mia, I'll always have love for you but my heart is no longer with you."

"WHAT?" She shouted and I moved the phone away from my ear.

"Consider that night, my closure."

"Closure?"

"Yea, closure. I thought, I did something wrong back in high school to make you cheat on me, but I realized, it's the ho in you."

"Excuse me!"

"Dennis is no longer here and his money must've run dry. You assumed, we'd reconnect and everything would be good."

"I would never do that Marco."

"I'm here to tell you, I'm done feeling like you

cheating, was my fault. I thought maybe,

I neglected you, when I was hustling but you were right there

with me, most nights. Then I thought, we didn't have enough

sex but we had a lot of it. I'm not sure why you did it and I no

longer care. I risked my relationship with a good woman,

thinking with my dick."

"Marco, please."

"Goodbye, Mia." I hung the phone up. You could hear

her screaming my name.

"Welcome another stalker." Tech, tipped his beer up to

sip.

"I know." I sat on the couch and continued watching

the baseball game with him. Ang, made us some chicken wings

and finger sandwiches.

"Give her time, Marco. She forgives everyone." Ang,

said and sat next to Tech.

"I hope so, Ang. I don't wanna live without her." I

picked my phone up and looked at the text.

My Rak: *I forgive you for hurting me because I don't like to have hate in my heart. However, you broke it and right now, I need space. I'm not saying we'll ever be together again, but I want us to be friends.*

Me: *I'll take anything you give me. Just don't leave me.*

My Rak: *Goodnight.*

Me: *I love you*

My Rak: *I love you too*

I smiled when she text it back. I put the phone in the clip and got comfortable. I didn't wanna stay on the estate without Rak and it was lonely as hell, in my other house. Tech and Ang, were gonna get tired of seeing me because I'm not leaving, until my girl and I, were together again.

Mia

I slammed my cell on the table, after Marco hung up on me. How could we have the perfect night and day; only for him to tell me, it was his closure? He should've had closure, years ago. Granted, I never had it but who needs it anyway. When a relationship is over, you don't need to consummate, one last time for fucking closure. I know the retard has everything to do with it and she's gonna pay for taking him from me. I mean, what can she actually have, that I don't. My body is banging, my sex is definitely off the chain and he loves my head game. She's too young to know how to do any of it, unless she's a ho. Now, that I think of it, Cara did say she stole Marco, from her.

I got up off the couch and opened the door. Someone was banging on it, for dear life and I know it wasn't Tech this time, since his boy isn't here. I opened it and sucked my teeth. These two idiots were at my door looking homeless. They came in and Zaire was limping. He sat down and before I could ask, he started telling me how Marco, killed his mother, set her on fire in the house and shot him. He was supposedly here to get revenge but my ex, isn't someone you walk up to and kill. Its gonna take some planning and extra hands on deck.

Shana came in bitching about Tech, not fucking with her because of his wife. I had to look at her, to see if she was serious. A man, won't allow you to fuck with his wife and even if he would still fuck her, she messed up by telling. All side chicks know, to keep their mouths shut. It's obvious she didn't know her position; otherwise, she'd still be bedding him. Sometimes, I wanna ask Marco, if he's really into this chick, could we still be friends with benefits. Then I thought about the time I was at the house with Bobbi and heard her ask. He'd curse me the hell out like he did her. Therefore, I had to devise a different plan and these two, are just the ones to help me. Oh, and Bobbi and Cara, could do a little something too.

The two of them were obsessed over Marco and I could see why. He was way beyond rich, his sex game is the best in the world and he's a boss. The type of BOSS that demands attention, before he even steps out the car. The kind who will have you killed with one look. Also, the kind who can wipe your entire family out, in an hour. Yes, this task will be risky but I'm willing to put in the work and get rid of this Rakia bitch. Even if I have to trick them, in believing he'll choose one of them, if she does die.

"Listen, we have to get rid of Rakia. If anything happens to her, he'll lose focus. It's when we'd be able to hit him hard." Zaire said and it made sense.

"Aren't you in love with her?" Shana asked and slipped her sneakers off.

"I used to be but not anymore. She's the one who had him come to Connecticut and kill my mother. Do you know, I can't even give her a funeral because I'm sure, they'll show up just to kill me?" I shook my head. He was right about that. They were most likely waiting, for him to set one up.

"I think we should figure out a way to lure Rakia, out the house and straight to Zaire. She seems to be gullible and Cara said, she is very forgiven." I told them and they agreed.

"Oh shit, look." Zaire pulled his phone out and showed us a video of him fucking her.

"Did he see this?" I asked and we waited for him to answer.

"Yup. It's the reason he came looking for me. I thought, I wouldn't be able to get it back but the chick went to my car and got the stuff, I left in there. I even sent it out in an email to spread but somehow he had a guy plant a virus on the computer and anyone who opened it up, lost everything on theirs."

"Well, it looks like he didn't delete it from your phone."

"I don't think he could because its in my phone as a video and not an email attachment. He'd have to get my phone, to delete it." The smile on my face, got wider.

"What you thinking?"

"How about we send this to her and say if she doesn't meet with you, you'll send it to the school? That way, she'll be so upset and try to stop you, she'd do anything. Once she shows up, we can snatch her up and hold her for ransom." They both looked at me.

"Tried that already and he hung up on me."

"If I know Marco, it's probably because he thought you were sleeping with her and she was in cahoots with you. But now, we know how head over heels, he's in love with her and won't do it again. He'll listen and give us whatever we ask for." Shit, if he won't be with me, I may as well get money outta him.

"Fuck it." Zaire shrugged his shoulders and so did Shana.

"What about Tech?"

"What about him?"

"I want him back."

"You don't have pictures, videos or anything of you two?" She shook her head no.

"Wait! The club is his, therefore he has a website. Get some photos off of it and have them photo shopped in pictures with you. Women do it all the time. She won't know, if its real or not." I could see her thinking.

"Don't get stupid with the photos."

"Huh?"

"Don't put his head on a body, you know don't look like his. You know, how people will put a light skinned person's head, on a dark ass body. The profile has to be perfect."

"I know right."

"Go home and take photos in your bedroom and other places in the house. Then screen shot some of him, off the website and go from there."

"Who can I get to do them?"

"Go online and type it in the search engine, of the internet. People will respond and hit you back. The good thing is, you can send them the photos from your phone, instead of having to drop them off."

"This is gonna be so much fun." She rubbed her hands together.

"Mia, I need you to go and grab what you can from Connecticut."

"Say what?" I gave Zaire a crazy ass look.

"Mia, you owe my mom and Dennis."

"Owe them?"

"Yea. We both know my brother died because of you."

"How you figure?"

"Well, if you and him, never went behind Marco's back and fucked around, they'd still be friends and we wouldn't be going through this. Then, you gave my nephew up for adoption, the minute he died and didn't tell any of us." I fell back on the couch.

I never meant to give my son up but the money was running low. I'm talking, I went from five million dollars when Dennis died, down to ten thousand, which is what's left in my bank account. Between plastic surgery and my shopping habit, I was tapped out. I went to the get a loan from the bank and because I never had credit cards, or any type of credit, they denied me. Unfortunately, the school my son went to, was expensive and the money was no longer there. I loved my son dearly but I never wanted a kid by Dennis.

Once Marco, disowned me, I knew he'd be my meal ticket, which is why, I kept the baby. He was ecstatic and couldn't wait for him to get here. I did have the mother instincts and treated my son, like the king he was. However, after Dennis died, I couldn't cope and said fuck it. My mother lived down south, in the country and had been asking me to bring my son there for years. Right before, coming here, I took him down there and let her adopt him. The papers had been drawn up and regardless, of how many times my mom tried to talk me out of it, I still did it. Getting Marco back, would be a task in itself, and having a kid around; especially one by his ex-best friend, would only complicate things. I planned on getting him back when Marco married me, which is still on my agenda. He's just confused right now but I'm gonna help him with that.

"My mother has him and we don't know, if he died over me."

"He may not have died because of you, but we all know, when Marco pulled the trigger, he still had hate in his heart, for what the two of you did." He was right. Even though Dennis tried to kill him first, once he saw Dennis, I'm sure he remembered what we did to him.

"Fine! What am I getting?" He gave me a list of things from his place and see, if there was anything left to retrieve from the house that burned. It probably wasn't. The way he made it seem, there's nothing left.

****

"Who are you?" Some chick asked when I was collecting things for Zaire.

"I'm Zaire's sister in law. Who are you?" She was a cute girl. A little thick but cute, nonetheless.

"Mary. I'm the one who helped him get outta town. Do you know where he is?" She looked sad.

"Yes. Thanks for helping him."

"Can you tell him, I'm pregnant and I need to know, what to do."

"Did you call him?"

"Yes, and he won't answer for me. I didn't do anything to him so I'm not sure, why he's ignoring me."

"He's probably nervous but I'll tell him for you. Are any of these things yours?" I lifted some women clothing and she shook her head no.

She stayed in the dorm room with me and helped with some bags, down the stairs. The heavier ones, I carried because

172

she's pregnant. By the time we finished, we had cleared out his drawers, collected school items, pictures and some papers he asked for. There was no laptop, which is unusual for a person who attends college. Maybe, the one he claimed Marco had a hold of, is the one he used. Who knows?

"I'll have him call you, or let him know what you told me." She gave me a hug and hopped in her car. After she drove off, I did the same but made a detour and went to the house his mom lived in.

I rode down the street and there was no house. The place was burned to the ground. You could tell, nothing was left to salvage. I got out the car and stood in front of it. This is the place, Dennis had me living in, until he was on his feet. His mom refused to move, when he had enough money. She loved this house, so I guess it made sense for her to die in it. It may sound harsh, but Marco may not have found her, if she moved.

"Who the fuck are you?" Some dude walked up, asking. He was handsome and you can tell he was street.

"No one."

"No one, huh. Then why you here at this rapist house?"

"Rapist?"

"Exactly! The dude who used to stay here with his mom, raped my Boss's girl and then kidnapped her. I can't wait to find him. That million dollars is gonna look perfect in my bank account."

"There's a reward for him?"

"Yup."

"Wow! He must've really pissed your boss off."

"He did. But look shorty, let me get your number."

"I have a man, thanks. See you later." I jumped in my car and called Zaire up.

"You raped Rakia?"

"Hell no!" He explained what he did.

I made him, send me the video from his phone and sat there watching. I never watched the entire thing, yesterday at my house, when he stopped by. Looking at it now, made me think differently of him. Even though he didn't rape her through penetration, he definitely did in another way. Whichever way he's looking at it, to make himself feel better, is his shit. At the end of the day, he had no business forcing her to do anything. I may not like her but no, means no.

I never called him back and drove to Jersey with a lot on my mind. Do I tell Marco where he is, and get the reward, or do I help them bring him down? I had so many questions in my mind but the motive is money and either way, I'd get some. *Decisions! Decisions!*

Angela

I was sitting in the nail salon with Rakia, minding my own business, when these two bitches walked in. Shana looked at me and the Mia, bitch stared at Rakia. Of course, she was nervous but I wasn't and waited for the two ho's, to come start trouble. She wanted to text Marco and I asked her not to. She started speaking to him a week after he went to her house and apologized. She still won't let him come around her. Not because she's scared but more or less, she thinks, she'll sleep with him and be right back in the same situation, with the women. I told her, whether she was with him or not, they'd still bother her because she had Marco, wrapped around her finger. She tried to debate it but we all knew better. Even his mom said, she's never seen him as smitten as he is with anyone, as he is with her. Mia, may have been the first woman he loved but Rakia, is the only one he gave a child too; twice. In my eyes, it meant something and I think she was starting to see it.

Anyway, the lady had just finished doing my feet and Rak, was still getting her nails done. The two of them, continued to stare and laugh but neither said a word. I know, they were conspiring to hurt one of us and I was waiting on it. Tech and I, were solid as could come and Marco, wasn't in a relationship with Rakia, so if he were doing something, it had nothing to do with her.

We were on our way out the door, when it started. I told Rakia, to prepare herself for the bullshit.

"I thought Marco and I, fucked liked rabbits but damn, you and Tech be going in. Didn't you say he was married?"

"Yea but what she don't know, won't hurt her." They started laughing. Rakia gave me a sad look. I doubt anything she said was true but I entertained her anyway.

"Hey ladies." They gave me a fake smile. Mia, gave Rakia an evil glare.

"It seems like you're discussing my husband and it wouldn't be right, if you didn't include his wife." I smirked and Shana stood up.

"Well, since you were being nosy. Me and my friend here, were looking at the photos of me and Tech. The ones, we took recently." Now I was lost because, to my knowledge, he hadn't seen her. He even fired her from the club.

"Yea, right."

"Take a look for yourself."

I snatched the phone from her and swiped through at least ten photos. Tech was in all of them. They were in a living room, the club and one in the bathroom. You couldn't see him clearly in one but she was naked. I'm assuming the shadow in the background, was him taking her picture. It was steamy, so the face was blocked out. I sent each picture to my phone and deleted my number out, before she could get it. I handed her the phone back and smiled.

"It looks like he has been spending time with the help, after all."

"Help? No miss. I'm the mistress, who he won't leave alone. This pussy will always keep him coming back." I didn't want to give her the energy but she asked for it.

"Shana, it's obvious my husband has you strung out. His sex game is very good but let me tell you this." I stepped closer.

"I promise to get to the bottom of these photos and if they are indeed real, you can have him, after I whoop your ass for sleeping with a married man. Tootles." I said and left her standing there with her mouth hanging open.

"RAKIA!" Mia yelled and we kept walking.

"Get in the car Rak."

"BITCH, I KNOW YOU HEAR ME."

"I don't have anything to say to you." Rakia got in the car and locked the door. Unfortunately, the window was down a little.

"Are you pregnant?" Rak, looked at me.

"Yes, I am." All of a sudden, Mia pulled her hair and started punching her. I sped off and Mia, fell in the street. I could've gotten out and beat her up but she would've gotten more hits off, and right now, Rak's nose was bleeding and she was crying.

"This is the exact reason, we can't be together. Everywhere I go, some woman is trying to attack me." I sat there quiet and handed her some napkins out the glove compartment. She was right. Marco had to control his ho's.

I parked in front of her condo and helped her get out. She was just turning five months and her stomach was showing but not enough where Mia, should've noticed. Rakia, had on an oversized shirt, which meant, Mia had to be staring hard as hell. She opened the door and went straight to the bathroom. I took my phone out to call Tech. He was out with Marco, as usual, but he would answer anytime his wife called.

"What's up sexy?" He made me smile. It turned into a frown when I opened the pictures.

"When's the last time you saw Shana? Matter of fact, when's the last time you slept with her?"

"What?"

"You heard me."

"Ang, the last time we did anything, was the night in the club, when you caught me. We saw her at the bar but I haven't seen her since. What's this about?"

180

"Check your phone." I hung up and waited for him to call me back.

"Is your memory refreshed?"

"Where are you? I need to talk to you." I broke down crying and hung up. Him asking to see me, only verified Shana's story. Why wouldn't he say no or she's lying; something? I checked on Rakia and told her, I'd call her later. She locked up behind me and I drove to my parents' house.

****

"How's my baby?" I picked lil Antoine up, off the floor. He was starting to crawl and loved being able to move around on his own.

"What's the matter?" My mom, came in asking. She and I, have been getting closer, ever since Tech, yoked her ass up. She hasn't laid a hand on me or even disrespected me in anyway.

"He's cheating."

"How do you know this?" She listened as I explained everything to her and sucked her teeth, afterwards. She stood up, grabbed a photo album and came to sit by me.

181

"I'm about to tell you a story and I hope you listen and learn." I nodded.

"It was about twenty-two years ago, when I met your father." I smiled. Some of their stories were funny.

"He was a jokester, street hustla and the most handsome man, I ever laid eyes on. Girl, when I tell you, he had me feeling things, no other man could, believe it." She had a huge smile on her face.

"Really!" I loved my dad but he was corny in my eyes.

"Really! Anyway, I used to see him all the time, and ignored the cat calls and ignorant comments the other guys would make because I only wanted him. He didn't speak and I never wanted the others, to assume I was interested because I entertained their foolishness." The doorbell rang and my mom, asked my dad to get it.

"One day, he came over to me and asked for a date. Of course, it took me all of two seconds to agree."

"Where did he take you?"

"Chile, to the damn arcade."

"The arcade?"

"Evidently, he was in a contest, with the pool game. He said, I was his lucky charm. Needless to say, he won and we went to celebrate at the pizza parlor. There were tons of people there, so we found a corner table with less distractions. That night, your father wooed himself in my life." I smelled my husband's cologne and turned to see him standing there. I rolled my eyes and listened to my mom finish.

"We became the couple everyone envied. We had been together for two years and things were perfect. Well, to me they were but not Gerrie.

"Gerrie, my mother?" I noticed my father tense up, as he leaned on the wall.

"Gerri, came to me one night and said, your father cheated on me." I covered my mouth. My mom told me many great stories of her and my dad but never this one, she was about to say.

"I didn't believe her and he said, she was lying." My father came further in the room and sat on the chair.

"I was pregnant at the time and felt like Gerri was jealous, which is why, she fed me lies about your father. A few months later, I find out; he was indeed cheating on me."

"How did you find out?" I could see how glassy her eyes were getting.

"I walked in on him, having sex with Gerri; in my bed."

"DAD!" I yelled out and he put his head down.

"I was devastated and so stressed out, I started hemorrhaging really bad. Instead of telling him about the pain, I left and went straight to the hospital; where I lost my daughter."

"How far along were you?"

"Seven months." I shook my head and felt Tech, come sit next to me.

"Because I was already stressing about him cheating; seeing them in bed, made it worse. Your father and Gerri, hurt me so bad, my baby couldn't take the pain. From that day forward, I left him and it took months for me to take him back. However, had I known he got the bitch pregnant, I never would've given him another chance." I felt some kind of way she called my mom a bitch but I understood.

"Why didn't you have more kids?"

"After you were born, I vowed to never have kids again. I didn't want to explain, why they had different parents. Call me selfish but your father was selfish when he stepped out and had a baby by someone else. Why should I give him one, when he's the reason, I lost the first one?" She was crying and so was my father.

"Why did Gerri do that to you?" She opened the photo album and started showing me pictures of two girls. They were cute and one looked like me as a baby. I assumed she was my mom.

"So, you two were best friends? It looks like the two of you did everything together." I flipped through the photos. She looked at my father.

"She was my sister." I stood up and the album fell off my lap.

"No, no, no. You can't be my aunt because you're my mother. Dad, tell me it's a mistake. My mom, wouldn't do her sister like that."

"Ang." My father tried to come to me and I backed away.

"How could you do that to her? She could've been my mother."

"Angela, she is your mother." My father said, staring at me pace the floor.

"I know but she could've been my birth mother. After she had her other daughter, you could've gotten her pregnant again and she would've been my mother. You gave away your sperm to a woman, who obviously wanted to be her. But her sister dad, how could you?" He didn't say a word.

"Ang, I didn't tell you the story to make you upset with your father. I told you because if you keep allowing this woman to cause havoc in your marriage, you're going to lose him." I stopped and stared at her.

"What does that have to do with my marriage?"

"Honey, Gerri hated the relationship he and I, had. Every chance she got, she told me things he was doing. True or not, it caused a lot of arguments and time away from each other. I'm not saying he was right for sleeping with my sister but I pushed him in the arms of another woman and didn't even know it. Ang." She sat me down on the couch.

"She may not be your sister or even a friend but she is someone, who wants your husband. Stop letting her get you upset. Your husband has done nothing but showed how much he loves you and you keep letting her separate y'all. Honey, always believe your man over a bitch off the street, until he shows you different."

"Ma, I'm sorry for being disrespectful to you all these years and.-"

"Ang, you were a kid and that's what they do. I apologize for smacking you, after finding out you were pregnant but I wanted better for you. I'm not saying he wasn't no good but at the time, I felt you were throwing your life away, your dad and I worked hard for you to have. Ang, whether you came from my womb or not, you're my daughter. My blood runs through you, regardless." I nodded my head.

"Why are you still with him?"

"ANG!" Tech yelled.

"No, its ok. Ang, I chose to stay because regardless of his mistake, I was madly in love with him. Not only that, it took me a while to forgive him and to this day, he's never cheated again, as far as, I know." My dad shook his head no.

"Or, it could be, he never cheated again because, I stabbed him in the stomach for cheating in the first place, but that's neither here nor there." She said it all non chalant.

"WHAT?" My dad shrugged his shoulders.

"You better not stab me." Tech said and I turned around and smirked.

"All I'm saying is, you two love each other and people don't like to see others happy. Instead of giving her what she wants by making you angry. Show her, how strong the union you two have, really is. One thing a bitter woman hates, is for you to continue being happy, even after she tried to break you."

"But she.-"

"I don't care what she showed you. Your husband is right there. Let him explain his side first and then make a choice on if you want to be with him, or if you want to keep believing the outsider." She stood next to my father and he pulled her down on his lap. She started giggling like a school girl.

"Thanks for the talk mommy." I hugged her, apologized to my dad and walked out with my husband. We had a lot to discuss and it started with getting rid of Shana.

Tech

Listening to the story about Ang's parents, had me in shock. Her mom always told me not to judge her off the bad stories, I may have heard. I'm not saying Ang, ever spoke bad about her, but she did say they didn't get along because she felt, her mom was too hard on her. Who knew, the woman she's been calling mom, all this time, is really her aunt? I definitely, gave her credit for sticking around after a miscarriage, an outside child and raising another woman's kid. Most women, would've walked away. However, her love for him outweighed all of it and I really hope Ang, learned from it. Not that I'm cheating but Shana is miserable as fuck and trying everything in her power to split us up.

We got home that night and Ang, wanted to discuss the photos and I didn't. Of course, she said they must be real, if I didn't. I showered, ate me some take out and laid in the spare room with my son. She can accuse me all she wants but one things for sure and that is, she ain't leaving me. I let her rant all night and even listened to her cry about me not giving her attention. In my eyes, she was being a spoiled brat and I'll speak to her, when I'm ready. Like her mother said, never listen to an outsider who wants her man and Shana, has been doing everything to destroy us, since the moment we met. I really thought Ang, was over the other shit but maybe she's not.

****

"Tech, Marco is here." She came in the room, damn near naked. Booty shorts and a tank top, is all she had on.

"And you answered the fucking door like that?" I hopped out the bed fast as hell. She had the nerve to smirk.

"He's not here. I wanted you to talk to me." I pushed passed her and went to use the bathroom.

"What, Ang?"

"I should be the one mad." I flushed and started the shower. How the hell should she be mad, when I'm the one, who's being accused of false shit?"

"I didn't tell your ass, to get in here." She knew my dick would get hard, looking at her.

191

"Well, I needed to shower too." She bit her lip and lifted her leg to wash.

"You could've washed before me."

"I could've but it's fun, when my husband is in here."

"You wanna play?" I lifted her up and slammed her down on my dick.

"Ahhh fuck, Tech."

"Nah, you wanna believe another bitch over your husband and then, act like a brat. I'ma give you, exactly what you want." I slammed her back against the wall and pumped harder. Her nails were in my back, as she sucked down hard on my neck.

"I'm sorry, Tech. Fuck, I'm cumming." I waited until she finished and went back at it.

"You're not sorry. Bend the fuck over." I let her down and she did what I asked.

"Throw it back, dammit." I smacked her ass harder and she came again. I continued fucking the hell out of her. When we finished, she whined that she was sore and couldn't walk.

"I bet your ass, won't listen to that bitch, no more."

"Fuck you." She said quietly. I heard her and ran to the side of the bed.

"Say it again."

"No." She pulled the covers over her head.

"That's what I thought. My pussy better be wet, when I get home too."

"Tech, no more today."

"Too bad. Soak in the tub or something. I'll be back later." I took the covers off her face and kissed her cheek.

"Tech, how did she get those photos?"

"Ang, if you took the time to pay attention, you'd see they were photo shopped. Each picture is straight off the website. Duh, I was fully dressed in each one. The shower photo, definitely ain't me. Look closely, it may be steamy in there but dude don't have hair and your husband has dreads. Ang." I sat her up.

"I would never cheat on you again. I couldn't take you leaving me for those three months. I also know, you won't take me back. I can't and won't risk you trying to leave me. And I say trying because you wouldn't make it out the house." She sucked her teeth.

"Try it and see." She stuck her tongue out. I leaned in and stuck mine, in her mouth.

"I'm sorry, Tech. She really knows how to get under my skin."

"I bet. Stop letting her though because all you're doing is making her believe, I may be cheating and she has a chance." She nodded. I lifted her head up.

"I don't want anyone but you."

"Same here." I stood up to leave.

"Oh. Mia, saw Rakia and knows she's pregnant. She came to the car and hit Rak, a few times in the face."

"WHAT? Why didn't you say something yesterday? That nigga gonna flip." They may not be together but he won't allow anyone to touch her.

"Rakia, asked me not to. She thinks Marco will kill her and she doesn't want anyone's death on her hands. Bad enough, Zaire called and threatened to kill her because Marco, killed his mom."

194

"Yo, what the fuck? You should've told me. The nigga is in town, which means, he's plotting on her. I gotta go." She came running behind me.

"Tech, I'm sorry. She said, she was telling Marco, when y'all got back from Connecticut, since that's when he called."

"Ang, that was weeks ago."

"I know and I thought she did but I'm guessing, she didn't." I walked towards her at the bottom of the stairs.

"Ang, I'm trying to figure out who tried to kill and run you off the road, and here the two of you, not once mentioned this nigga threatening her. What if he got her? What if he sent someone to get both of you? Next time, think baby. Don't let Rak, say she's gonna mention something because we all know she isn't."

"I promise, to tell you everything from here on out." I kissed her again and headed out the door. I hit Marco up, once I got in my car.

"Where you at?"

"At the mall with ma, buying all this shit for the baby."

195

"Rak, is gonna kill you. She said not to buy anything until she's six months."

"I told her but she said, she'll keep it at the house until then. Man, you know I can't control when she shops." I laughed because he was right. His mom stayed in the mall, outlets and anywhere else, a person could spend money.

However, she was very excited about Rak, having her second grand baby. Yes, she considered my son, her first. Between her and Ang's parents, we barely ever had him, though. Let her tell it, I'm the only one she expected to have kids because Marco was a ho and too mean. She also felt, Mia would've been the only one to give them to her. That went out the window, when the ho cheated.

I know people may think, I'm bugging for calling her out. But I was the one who saw how hurt he was. Yea, the nigga shed tears over her. He planned on marrying her and having a family. If you're wondering; no, he never cheated either. After he found out about the affair, he turned into a ho. Then became a beast in the streets. His heart turned cold and nothing else mattered; until Rak, came in his life. She was a breath of fresh air for him and he loved everything about her.

I see how hard he's fallen for Rakia and I understand. It took him eight years to find, who he calls, his true soulmate and he messed up, fucking with Mia. I admit, I was shocked he got Rakia pregnant but after meeting her; again, I understood. Rak, was laid back, quiet, funny in her own way and loved the hell outta him. The love was and still is, seen in her eyes and written on her face. He's stressing like crazy without her. I know exactly how he feels because when Ang left me, I was the same way. We all know, she's gonna give him another chance but I think she's making him work to get her back. Ang, said she's gonna make sure he knows, not to ever cheat again.

"Come see me at the club, when you finish."

"Aight."

****

"I said meet me at the club, nigga. Do this look like the club?" I closed the door behind him. It was almost midnight and his ass was just getting here.

197

"I went, duh! They told me you left for the night." I didn't stay at the club late because I never wanted my wife to feel like, either I was cheating, or neglecting my family.

"What Ang cook? I'm hungry." He walked in the kitchen and opened the fridge.

"You always hungry."

"Ma, thinks I'm having the pregnancy symptoms." He shrugged his shoulders and took the pot of spaghetti out. I sat down while he scooped the food out, placed it in the microwave and grabbed something to drink. I had to figure out how to break it to him, about Mia.

Once he sat down, I started discussing the dumb shit, Shana did and how Ang, believed her. He was shocked to hear about her parents. I can't lie, the entire story threw me for a loop. They still looked happy though. I think Ang's mom was trying to tell her, men mess up but it doesn't mean you can't move past it, and be happy. After we talked about the new shipment coming in and the new people who wanted to cop from him, he looked at me.

"What aren't you telling me?" This nigga always knew when I was hiding something. Instead of telling him, I ran upstairs and threw on some sweats, sneakers and grabbed a jacket.

"Where you going?" Ang asked flipping the covers off and showing me how naked she was. I licked my lips and ran over to her.

"Damn baby. I have to tell Marco, about Mia and Zaire. He's gonna wanna kill them."

"I guess, she'll be ready when you get home." She tried to stick her hand in between her legs and I popped her.

"That's me all day. I got you." I covered her back up and ran down the steps. Marco, was on the couch flipping through the channels.

"What the fuck you get dressed for? We going back out?" He stood up.

I started telling him what happened and the nigga, flew past me. I yelled up the steps for Ang, to come lock the door and ran to my car. He didn't even wait for me. *Some brother he is.* This nigga sped, in and outta traffic. I thought he was going to Mia's but he went to Rak's. He jumped out with me right

behind him. If he came here first, it was for a reason.

Rakia

I was deep in my sleep, when someone started banging. The only person who would do this, is my baby daddy but why is he here this late? We spoke before I went to bed and everything was fine. He and I, spoke all the time on the phone now but I still wouldn't allow him to come over.

The way he's going on, it's like something's wrong. I grabbed my robe, put on my slippers and walked down the steps slowly. I had the phone in my hand, just in case it wasn't him. I looked through the peephole and sure enough, it was Marco. The look on his face, made me ask, if he were ok.

"I'm good, ma. Open the door." I unlocked it and once it opened, his entire facial expression changed. I mean, my nose was swollen and I had a black eye, but I didn't say anything to him because I knew, he'd be upset, like he is now. He grabbed my hand and took me in the room.

"Put some clothes on."

"Huh."

"Get dressed. I need you to take a ride with me."

"Marco, its late and.-"

"Ma, I'm not gonna ask you again."

"Tech, what's going on?"

"Rak, please just get dressed."

"FINE!" I pouted and pulled some sweats out, a sweat shirt and slid on my Ugg slippers. I stood there waiting for him to say something else but all he did was stare.

"Whatttt? Is something wrong with my clothes because I can change them? Do you want me to?-" I was about to ramble and he shushed me with his lips.

"Ummm. Marco, you know we're not a couple. Why would you kiss me?" He grabbed my hand and led me out the door and into his car. Once he closed it, he ran on the other side to get in.

"You already know where I'm going." He said to Tech, who nodded.

We drove for a good twenty minutes and stopped in front of another set of condos. They were pretty nice and the neighborhood looked quiet. He came around, opened the door

202

for me and we walked up the steps together. Tech, was behind me, shaking his head. I waited for him to knock and instead of doing it, he kicked the door off the hinges. The place was dark, so he flipped the light on. Some chick came running out the room and that's when I realized, he knew, she's the one who did this to my face. I'm gonna kill Angela for telling Tech, who I know, told him.

"You did this to her face?" Mia stopped dead in her tracks and looked at me. I backed up, into Tech.

"She won't touch you." Marco walked over to her and punched her so hard in the face, you could hear her nose crack. I covered my mouth.

"Come here, Rak."

"Marco, I don't want any parts in this."

"COME HERE!" He shouted and Tech pushed me towards him.

"Marco, can we go?"

"You did this to her face Mia?" At first, she wouldn't answer, so he yanked her by the hair. She nodded.

"I'm sick of you stupid bitches coming for her, when I'm the one, who chose her. She doesn't fuck with any of you. Matter of fact, the easiest way to end this, is to kill all of you." Mia shook her head no, over and over.

"Marco, its ok."

"It's not ok. They keep fucking with you because I don't want them." He pulled his gun out and placed a connector or something to it. He put it on her temple.

"MARCO!"

"She needs to go Rak, or its going to keep happening."

"Marco, please don't kill her. I'll do whatever you want."

"Whatever I want." I shook my head yes. He had a sinister grin on his face and Tech, stood behind me laughing. It was like this man, had an idea in his mind already. I wouldn't put it past his sneaky ass.

"Are you gonna give me another chance?" I sucked my teeth and rolled my eyes.

"Something else."

"That's all I want." Blood was gushing from Mia's nose and he pressed the gun back on her temple.

"Marco, you cheated on me."

"It won't ever happen again." I didn't know what to do. He was holding a gun to the woman, who punched me in the face for being pregnant, by him. Then, he wanted to bargain and make me say yes, to being with him. Should I take him back? It has been a few months and he's been stalking me ever since. Maybe he did learn his lesson.

"Time is ticking, Rak." His finger was on the trigger and I could see him pulling it back. Mia's eyes were so big.

"Rak, hurry up. My wife, is sending me nasty messages. I need to get home."

"Ummm." I felt so much pressure.

"Fuck it. I'll just kill her." He really didn't give a shit about Mia anymore, if he could put a gun to her head and be ready, to pull the trigger.

"NO!" I shouted and he looked at me.

"Well?" He questioned with a big ass grin on his face. I hated to be in this predicament but I didn't want anyone's death on my hands.

"Ok, ok. I'll take you back but if you cheat again, I promise, to never speak to you." He stood up and kissed me deeply.

PHEW! PHEW! I heard and looked down. Marco, shot her in the stomach and leg. It looked like a horror movie, where blood starts gushing out of the person's body.

"You said, you wouldn't kill her." I stormed away.

"She's not dead." We both looked at her.

"Yet!" He shrugged his shoulders and led me out the door. This man is a maniac. What did I get myself into? My baby better not come out like him.

****

"Why did you do that and where are we going?" He ignored me and kept driving. We pulled into his house and he told me, he'd be right back.

"What's in there?" I asked about the duffle bag, he tossed in the back seat.

"Oh, that's my clothes, toothbrush, pajamas and other stuff. Unless you don't want me to sleep in pajamas. I can leave them in the truck.

"Why do you have all of it?"

"Because we're back together and I'm not spending another night, without you." I smiled and he lifted my hand to his lips.

"I swear, on our kid and future kids, to never cheat on you again Rak. If you wanna check my phone every day, go online and look at my phone bill, to see who I call, come with me when I leave the house, or anything else, just so I can prove, I'll never cheat. Let me know. I don't ever wanna lose you again." By the time, he finished the little short statement, my ass had tears in my eyes. It wasn't what he said, but how he said it. It was sincere and real. We drove the rest of the way, in silence.

"I'm taking a shower." He said when we got in my condo. I locked everything up and brought him a towel in the bathroom. Why did I do that? I could see his frame from the glass door and it's a shame, a man could be as sexy, as he is.

"Stop staring and get in." I jumped. How did he know, I was here?

"I was bringing you a towel." He opened the glass door and pulled me close. I let him remove all my clothes and help me in.

"Damn, you're beautiful pregnant. I never thought you'd allow me to witness my baby in your belly, this way." He bent down and kissed it. He's right. I never told him when the appointments were and we only spoke on the phone. Ang, would give him the ultrasound pictures for me and if he tried to facetime me, I'd deny the call. Now, we're standing here eye to eye and no one is saying a word.

"Let me wash you up." He lathered the rag and took his time. When he finished, he stood me under the shower and rinsed the soap off. I felt his lips touch my neck and closed my eyes.

"Marco." I moaned out.

"Yea, babe." His hands were massaging my breasts.

"I want to be craved by you." He stopped and stared.

"I want you to think about kissing and touching me, as much as, I think about, kissing and touching you. I want you to wake up, wanting me, like I want you." He lifted my face.

"I've craved you, for a very long time, ma. The cravings were bad, when you didn't fuck with a nigga. Now, that we're one again, I'm gonna continue craving you but this time, you'll be right next to me." I looked into his eyes and they were so sincere.

"Marco."

"Yea."

"Make love to me." He shut the water off and helped me out the tub. We stepped in the room and he laid me down, gently.

He kissed my entire body, from head to toe and I enjoyed every minute of it. My legs were opened and spread apart, as his tongue found its way to my protruding treasure. It felt like there was a heartbeat because it was ready to burst. He sucked on it and just like that, I exploded in his mouth and he didn't let any of my juices drop. I sat up and watched him devour me, like lunch and grabbed his hair. My bottom half begin to grind on its own, and I was fucking the hell, outta his face. His hands were on my ass, as he pulled me closer. You would think he was trying to get inside my pussy.

"Yesssssss. Fuck Marco. Take it all." I yelled out. He stood up, wiped his mouth and tried to lay me down.

"I wanna do you."

"Nah. I'm good."

"Marco, please. I need to learn how to please my man."

"You already do. Lay back." I grabbed his dick and started stroking it. He didn't know what to do, at this point.

"Rak, I know what he did. You don't. Fuckkkkk!" He yelled out, once I put him in my mouth. He bit down on his lip, as I sucked, spit, used both hands to go up and down and even lifted his balls, to lick under there. All of a sudden, his body became very stiff and he grabbed the back of my hair.

"Ma, don't swallow. It's your first timeeeeeee. Ahhhh shittttttt." I swallowed and continued, until his dick went soft. He fell back on the bed and had me lay next to him.

"Rak, I swear before God, right now, I better be the only man you did that to."

"You are. But he.-" Marco sat up and told me, never to worry about him again and what he made me do, don't count.

"I'm not trying to cover up what happened to you and if you wanna see someone, we'll go together. But ma, I'm the only man, you've performed oral sex on and we're going to keep it that way." I nodded.

"Where did you learn how to do this? I know, it wasn't another man so which website?"

"Redtube."

"Redtube?"

"Yea. I tried to get into Pornhub, but none of the videos were good to me. You know, when you click on one site, a bunch of others pop up. I clicked on that one and learned. It took me a few tries with bananas. However, they didn't stay hard."

"Its all good. Now, let your man, make love to you, like you asked." I laid back and gave him access to what he's been waiting for.

"Warm and tight, the way it should be. We're about to have a long night, Rak." I pulled his face to mine and kissed him.

"We better. There's a lot of making up to do." He and I, did some nasty, freaky things to each other and passed out. It's been a long time coming but he's worth it.

Marco

"Fuckkkkk, Rak." I moaned out, as she took me in her mouth. Ever since she tried it a few weeks ago, she does it all the time. I appreciate the fuck outta her waking me up to head, but I keep telling her, she doesn't have to do it everyday. She claims to do it because we've been messing around for so long, and she's never tried. It was her way of making up for time missed.

"Shitttttt." I grabbed her hair and let go. She never let any of my soldiers drop.

"Damn, ma."

"Mmmmm, I love tasting you." She kissed my lips.

"And I love tasting you." I had her get on all fours, and attacked her pussy with my mouth. She loved for me to do it this way.

"Cum for me, Rak. I stuck two fingers inside and she leaked out, like a faucet.

"Yea, just like that." I stood up and entered her. We both moaned out in pleasure.

"I love you so much, Marco." I wrapped my hand around her throat and pulled her up, still moving in and out. I turned her to face me.

"I love you too baby." Our tongues danced with each other and that was it. We turned into animals and stayed in the house all day. She is definitely, worth giving up random pussy for.

****

"I'm hungry." She whined after we finished sexing each other down.

"What you want?"

"A nice California cheeseburger, with cheese fries and fried mushrooms." I shook my head and stood up to get in the shower. I had to go out anyway, so I may as well get it.

"Am I eating too much? Maybe, I should cut down." She stepped in the shower with me.

"Rak, you're six and a half months pregnant and even if you weren't and wanted to eat all day, I wouldn't care. Stop overthinking shit. I'm not ever leaving you. I'm in love with you and your size isn't a factor."

"Sooo, if I weighed six hundred pounds, you'd stay with me?" She grabbed the soap.

"Yup."

"You would?"

"We'd have to agree to an open relationship though."

"Why?"

"Because ain't no way in hell, I'm lifting all that skin up to fuck. And you can cancel me eating that good ass pussy." She busted out laughing.

After we washed up and got dressed, she got in her car to go by, Ang's. She gave me a hard time coming home and it took her a week, to agree. I paid the condo off and let her rent it out to someone, for income. She would never need money, but she was upset about having to take maternity leave already. Rak, is very independent and wanted her own. I understood, but she had to know, her man will always support her through anything. That's why, I opened an account and had a black card in her name. She refused to use the card, but its there.

When she saw the amount of money in her bank account, I had to yell at her, for trying to go in the bank and have it transferred back into my account. I only found out because the manager called and asked me, if I wanted that. I swear, she is a piece of work but at least, I knew she wasn't around for my money. Even if she were, I wouldn't care because she had my heart and no one, could take it from her. Not even Mia, who assumed, us fucking could take it. I guess she learned her lesson.

Now, all I had to do was find stupid ass Cara and Bobbi, oh and I won't forget the aunt. I'm sure my dad is hiding her out and its fine. All I have to do is go over there and he'll fuck up and tell me. I've been waiting to bring it up to Rak, because she loves her family. However, she knows Cara is a wrap; no if, and's or buts about it. The bitch may not have cut her real deep, but she had a small scar on her neck and arm. It doesn't bother me, but it reminds me of what the bitch did and she has to die; plain and simple.

"Call me, when you get there." I closed the door and stuck my head in the window for a kiss.

"I should be fine, with them behind me."

"Yea, but you never know." I thought about the people cutting the guard off, watching Ang and almost killed her.

"Ok. I love you and have a good day."

"Wait! You want me to bring the food to you over there?"

"No. I changed my mind. I want seafood." She shrugged her shoulders and pecked my lips again. She pulled off and I hopped in my truck. I picked up my phone, without looking and hated myself for doing so.

"Hello, Marco." I knew the voice.

"How did you get my number?"

"It was in Mia's phone. Can you meet me somewhere?"

"For what?"

"Please. I need to discuss some things with you."

"Where and I'm not staying long."

"I'm at the hospital." I blew my breath out because if this was a plot to keep me and her snake ass daughter together, she was about to get her feelings hurt.

"I'll be there in twenty minutes. Be downstairs waiting."

I called Tech and let him know, I'd be running late for our meeting. He knew how to run it, and didn't really need me. It was about getting Zaire and because we spoke every day, all day, I didn't have to be there. Shit, we knew the plan. It's the other ones, who we had to inform. Now, that the original guy who was feeding him information, is dead, we weren't worried about shit getting back. And if it did, we always had another plan.

****

I pulled up in the parking lot of the hospital and stepped out to see Ms. Connie, standing there waiting. She had the nerve to lick her lips. She was always a perverted woman and often, flirted with me, even at a young age. One time, I was fucking Mia from behind in her room and she opened the door. I let the bitch watch because Mia would've been upset, if she knew her mom did that. After that, I never fucked Mia in the house again, to keep the peace. It didn't stop her from wanting to fuck and right now, it doesn't look like she ever got over the fantasy.

"What up, Ms. Connie." She hugged me extra tight and I had to push her off.

"You look handsome as ever." I shook my head.

"I'm about to leave."

"Marco, I called you because Mia may not make it." I shrugged my shoulders and lit a black and mild.

"Do you even care what happens to her?"

"Nope." I blew smoke in her face.

"Ooook." She dragged the word out.

"Someone shot her in the stomach and leg." The reason she may not make it, is because not only did she lose a lot of blood waiting for an ambulance, the bullet was hollow point and fucked her insides up. I'm shocked she's lasting this long. I never told Rak that. She'd have a fit because she didn't want her death, on her hands.

"I did."

"WHAT?" She screamed out.

"Yea, she was fucking with my girl, who's pregnant and you know, I don't play that shit."

"Are you serious? You'll shoot your first love over some bitch." I threw my hands around her throat and whispered in her ear.

"If you ever speak ill, of my girl again. I promise, you'll be next to your daughter." She nodded and I let her go.

"Now, that I've made myself clear about my girl. What the fuck do you really want?" She rubbed her neck.

"I've had custody of Mia's son for a while now and if she dies, I'll be the one raising him. Do you think, you can set an account up for him?" I laughed hard as hell in her face.

"Bitch, are you crazy? Not only, is he not my son, your ho ass daughter cheated on me, with a nigga, I considered a brother and gave birth to his kid. Do you really think, I'd give him anything?"

"Marco, she didn't mean to cheat and he should be your son."

"If it happened once, I'd agree but they made a relationship out of it. Then, he got her pregnant and married her. So, don't tell me, she didn't mean it. Save that shit for someone who's stupid."

"I don't know what to do because.-"

"Because what? Dennis was taking care of you too, when he was alive, right? And when he died, knowing Mia, she spent his money up, which is why, she gave you custody. She knew, you didn't spend all your money because you've always taught her to save some for a rainy day. Now, you're running low and want me to come to the rescue. Am I right?" She looked at the ground.

One... I don't know the kid and don't care too. Had Dennis and I, been on good terms, or even Mia, I may have. Two... The little nigga ain't even mine. And third... My girl would kill me; especially, when she's having my kid. I'm supposed to take from my seed and future seeds, to take care of someone else's. You bugging."

"Marco, you have it."

"You're right, I do." My phone started ringing.

"Yea babe." I looked at Ms. Connie and the bitch was eyeing my dick. Rak, told me they were bringing her grandmother in because she passed out and they don't know why.

"I'm here already. I'll see you soon." I hung up and waited for her to say, what I knew she would.

"What do I need to do? I'm sure we can work something out." She put her hand on my chest and started rubbing. Just as I removed it, a truck pulled up in front of us and out stepped my girl. She looked as good as she did, when we parted ways, not too long ago.

"You don't have shit I want." My girl came over to me.

"Marco. Is she your aunt?" Rak asked and kissed me.

"No. This is Mia's mom, Ms. Connie. Connie this is my woman, Rakia." Rak extended her hand and she looked her up and down. I could see how confused Rak was.

"Don't shake her hand ma."

"Marco!"

"Nah ma. She just tried to fuck me, for money." Rak's mouth dropped open. Ms. Connie moved closer, lifted her hand to smack me and Rakia pushed her back; making her fall. My ass was shocked to see Rak, put her hands on anyone.

"Don't ever put your hands on my man. Take your nasty ass upstairs and say goodbye to your daughter, who probably won't make it." Rak, grabbed my hand and stepped over Ms. Connie. I kicked her dumb ass in the stomach.

"Stop Rak." I pulled her back and stared at her.

"Look at you, getting a little gangsta."

"Nobody will touch you; except me. She was trying to get free feels and all this." She ran her hand up and down my chest.

"Is all me."

"Damn Rak. Can we go in the bathroom real quick, so you can handle this?" I let her feel how hard my dick was.

"Why are you hard? She better not had turned you on."

"HELL NO! You did this. Shit, you turned me on, being hood." She laughed.

"I got you later. I wanna make sure my grandmother is ok." I walked behind her.

"Stop switching Rak. I swear, I'll drag your ass in the bathroom." She turned around.

"I'm not switching, nasty. You just like the way, it moves."

"Hell yea, I do." She shook her head and walked on the side of me. It was better because I for sure, would take her in there.

We waited for about an hour before a doctor came out. He told Rak, her grandmother suffered a bad stroke and is in a coma. She may not make it, so it's best to get the family together and make arrangements. She was hysterical and the doctor made her go in another room, due to her blood pressure, elevating. I called my mom, Tech and Ang, and they were all on their way. Rak, whined about staying in the hospital because of the food. I asked Tech, to stop off and get her the damn burger and fries, she asked for earlier. Of course, he said, she need to stop eating. When he came in the room with Ang, she devoured the food and fell straight to sleep.

"Look at her fat ass." Ang said and we all laughed.

"Don't come for my girl." I mushed her in the head.

"Whatever. Did she see her grandmother?"

"Yea, it's the reason she's here."

"What you mean?" Tech asked and Ang sat on his lap.

"She had tubes everywhere and one time, they had to put us out because her heart stopped. They even called a code blue for a minute and then cancelled it."

"Damn." Tech shook his head.

"No matter what the case, you know she loved her grandmother. Shit, Rak, loves everyone but this is gonna hurt, if she doesn't make it. And right now, the pregnancy is ok, but I'm scared, she'll deliver too early." I put my head down and Ang, came to sit by me.

"Marco, I know its early, but she's passed the six-month mark. People deliver babies at five months and everything is fine. The baby may not be able to come home right away, but will survive. The NICU is made especially for premature babies." My mom walked in with Lil Antoine and he reached out for Tech. Ang, sucked her teeth.

"The next one, I'm spoiling."

"Yo, I know she's not pregnant again." He shrugged his shoulders.

"No. And if I was, what's the problem?" She had her hands on her hips.

"Because you were a pain in the ass."

"Oh, like Rak, is?"

"Didn't I tell you to stop coming for her."

"Well, if it isn't the man of the hour." I heard and looked up to see Shanta. She had my father with her, as if it meant anything. I stood up, Tech handed the baby to Ang and had her and my mom, stand in front of the bed.

"What the fuck you want?" I made my way towards her and she stood behind my pops.

"I came to see my niece." I reached around my father and yanked her up by the hair.

"Ahhhhh." She screamed and woke Rakia up. I was pissed because I was gonna drag her ass out and take her out, her misery.

"Marco, what's going on?" I let go and tossed her dumb ass to the floor.

"This bitch came in here to see you."

"How did you know where I was Shanta?" Rak, took my hand in hers. I think it was to keep me from killing her.

"I came to see my mother and they said her granddaughter was in the emergency room. I thought it was Cara." I chuckled.

"Bitch, you knew, her thot ass wasn't here."

"Marco, please. My grandmother is here and I just want some peace." I nodded and all of a sudden, we heard *Code Blue* over the intercom and all available doctors are needed, on the ICU floor.

"I have to get upstairs. Marco, what if it's my grandmother?" I took the blood pressure machine off her arm and bumped Shanta hard as hell. The bitch dramatically, fell into the wall. I asked the nurse to wheel Rak up, to check on her grandmother. I didn't wanna take the IV out.

The nurse came with a chair and we followed her. I gave the bitch Shanta, a death stare on the way to the elevator and Tech was cracking up. Ang, had to tell him to stop. My mom had lil Antoine in her arms and when Shanta tried to play with him, I thought she would die. Ang and my mom, gave her a look not to even think about it. She squeezed my father's hand tight as hell. I swear, if Rak wasn't here, she'd be dead in the alley, somewhere.

The nurse told us, only two can go in at a time. Rakia went in and Shanta tried but I cut it short. She would not be left alone with my girl, ever again. I made her stay right there, until we came out.

"There's her room." Rak pointed and her grandfather was standing there with tears coming down his face. We knew then, it was the end.

"NOOOOOOO!" Rak screamed out and her grandfather came running over. They hugged and he told her, everything was fine, one minute and the next, she was gone. Her grandmother, evidently had a DNR in place, so they didn't try to save her. They did on the way in because no one knew. Her grandfather said he did, but wasn't telling them shit, because he didn't agree with it.

"That's him, right there." We turned around and Shanta came walking with cops, in our direction.

"What up, Ronnie and Marcus? Its been a long time."

They gave me a half hug and I introduced them to Rak and her grandfather.

"This woman claims you attacked her."

"Word!"

"Shanta, why would you call the cops on him?" Everyone was looking in our direction. I asked the nurse to take Rakia and her grandfather, for a walk.

"Yes, you did and Rakia, don't you dare lie for him." She yelled as they walked away.

"What did he do, ma'am?"

"He grabbed my hair and tossed me on the floor. I want him arrested." Me and the cops busted out laughing. She was so fucking stupid. Didn't she know, I owned the police?

"What's so funny?" She had her arms folded.

"We came here, for an assault on a woman. Had we known, you were speaking of our BOSS, we would've never come."

"I don't care if he's the BOSS, he has to be arrested for yanking my hair and pushing me to the ground."

"Shanta, your mother just passed away and all you're worried about is some accusation you made up, to get me away from Rakia. Do you even care?"

"I know she died because my father was crying." She stood there with her arms folded.

"Ok, so comfort him. Take a minute out of your shitty life and think of what he's going through. That was his wife, the mother of his children, the woman, he planned on spending the rest of his life with. You dumb bitch; he just watched her take her last breath and you're in here making a fucking scene, over nothing. What the fuck is wrong with you?" She stood there looking stupid.

"Can y'all stay here for a few?" I asked Ronnie and Marcus.

"Yea, we'll go talk to Tech, or do you need us in here? We wouldn't want you to yank her hair or throw her to the ground." All three of us, busted out laughing.

"Nah, take her dumb ass outta here. Let the ones who really loved Mrs. Winters, grieve in peace." Shanta yelled obscenities the entire way out but once she put Rakia's name in her mouth, I had to remind her of who I was.

"I'm gonna ripped your vocal chords out, if you don't shut the fuck up." She looked at the cops who turned their heads.

"Let my girl name come out your mouth again and I promise you will be dead by morning. The only reason, I haven't done it yet, is because of Rak. But you got one more time, to come out your face and my girl will just be mad. Now, get the fuck outta here." She didn't say a word and walked out quiet, like I knew she would. *Fucking bitch.*

Rakia

"Do you think she was in pain?" I asked my grandfather, as we sat in my grandmothers' room. The nurses were unhooking the machines.

"Yo, can you do that shit, when they're finished? THA FUCK!" Marco, yelled out. Me and my grandfather snickered. He was a fool and had no filter.

"I'm sorry, I was just.-"

"Get the fuck out. Come back when they leave." The lady sucked her teeth but her ass left.

"No."

"What happened?" I stood up and Marco, came behind me.

"We were watching television and she said, she didn't feel good. I went to get her a bottle of water and came back to find her, face down on the floor. I called 911 and they revived her in the ambulance. What am I gonna do without her?" He started crying, which made me cry. My grandparents have been together for over forty years. All they knew, were each other.

"DAMMIT! I tried to get here in time." He yelled out and came towards me.

"Who the fuck are you?" Marco, pushed him back. He's never met my parents.

"He's my father." I put his arm down and hugged my dad.

"I should've been here. Ma, I'm so sorry for not getting my life together for you sooner. FUCK!!!!" He shouted and grabbed her hand. I stood back and watched him and my grandfather, say their goodbyes. They both left and it was my turn but where do I start?

"Grandma, I'm sorry, I wasn't there to say goodbye. I'm gonna miss you so much." I felt the tears falling down my face.

"Who am I gonna call, when your daughter and other grandchild bother me? Or who am I gonna talk to, when Marco, gets on my nerves?" He nudged me.

"You're gonna miss your great grandchild being born. How could you leave me alone?" Marco pulled me away, wiped my face with his sleeve and hugged me. This was the worst day in my life and all I wanted to do was curl up in a ball and die. My grandmother died, my aunt tried have my man arrested and I have a feeling my, dear sweet cousin, is going to come and try to harm me again. He kissed my forehead.

"Take me to the room please." He helped me in the chair and pushed me out. I told them, someone would call in an hour, with the name of the funeral home, who'd be picking her up.

My aunt was still in the waiting area, looking pitiful and my father and grandfather were talking on the side. My dad, came over and told me, they wanted me to handle all the arrangements and if I couldn't to let them know. Neither of them wanted Shanta doing anything but they would let her, if I didn't. She came walking over and I thought about kicking her for some reason.

"Why is she in charge? I'm her daughter?"

"And I'm her son. I'm the oldest and dad doesn't wanna do it. He wants Rakia to, since she was the closest to her."

"Fuck that. Cara, was closer to her." Was she really acting up, over me handling the services?

"Shanta can do it, if she wants to." She smirked.

"She was my wife and I say who handles, what? I don't want her doing it." My grandfather said and went to leave. Shanta ran behind him and he pushed her away.

"You may be my daughter but the sight of you is making me sick, to my stomach."

"Daddy."

"Your mother just passed, not even twenty minutes ago and all you're worried about is being in charge of the services. When is the last time you came to the house? Or the last time you called her? You let that daughter of yours attack my other granddaughter, and you said nothing. Your son doesn't even want you in his life but you wanna handle things. Shanta, get out of my face." She stormed off and my grandfather nodded at me, to do it. I was shocked because my grandfather didn't say much, and seeing him go off on her, let me know how much pain is was really in.

"We'll pay for everything?" Marco said and pushed the wheelchair, on the elevator.

"We?"

"Yes, we. My money, is your money. Spare no expense for her."

"Marco."

"I wish, you would say no." He wheeled me off the elevator and into my room. I got in the bed and one of the nurses came in, to hook me back up. My blood pressure was fine but I still had to stay. He shut the light off and climbed in bed with me. The two of us watched television, until we fell asleep. This is gonna be a hectic week.

****

"Look how sexy my baby mom is, dressed in black." Marco stood behind me and rubbed my stomach. We were at my grandmother's house waiting for the limo. I was not bringing any of them, to where I lived; except my grandfather and Rahmel.

"You think, I did a good job? I want to make sure everything is perfect for my grandmother. Did the people say, they'd have the doves? What about the food at the repast? Honey.-" He shushed me with his lips.

"Mmmmm. I needed that. Gimme some more." I wrapped my arms around his neck.

"We have time for a quickie." He asked kissing on my neck. I moved away, locked my old bedroom door and walked towards him.

"I could use one right now." I turned around and lifted my hair, so he could unzip my me. He slid the dress off my shoulders and began placing kisses down my back.

KNOCK! KNOCK! He didn't stop and I refused to make him. His tongue was literally at the top of my ass, when someone knocked again.

"Dammit." I whispered. He lifted the dress and zipped me back up.

"Why is there only one limo?" Shanta barked and stood there with her arms folded.

"Shanta, the limo is huge. It seats 15 and it's only me, Marco, daddy, you, Rahmel, his girl and grandpa. The one we got isn't necessary but at least everyone will be comfortable." My mother refused to come because she said, my grandmother blamed her, for my dad getting high. To be honest, I couldn't tell you, who got who, hooked.

"Why is he in the car?" I squeezed his hand.

"Grandma loved Marco and he's my man. Rahmel has his girlfriend coming and you don't seem to have an issue with her."

"That's because she doesn't wish death on me."

"Shanta, you attacked me for no reason. Then you destroyed my truck because he brought it. Do you think he'd let you get away with that? I'm his woman."

"What the fuck ever. Let's go." I grabbed her arm and she snatched it away.

"Shanta, what happened to you? You were my favorite aunt and always had my back. One day, you switched up on me and I don't know why. Even through, all of the bad things you did and said to me, I never hated you. Why do you hate me?" She looked at Marco.

"He's the reason, you and Cara are at odds."

"Shanta, you know that's not true. I know the first come, first serve rule. I was the one who saw him first. Cara was too busy talking to other guys, to even notice him. She's the one who didn't follow the rules."

"Well, if he didn't sleep with both of you, none of this would've happened."

"Marco, never sleep with Cara." She gave me a confused look.

"Oh no! Rak, he isn't who.-"

"Can we go now?" Marco said and grabbed my hand. Why did he cut her off and give her a hateful stare? I guess, I'll find out later because it's time for the services.

Throughout the service, I kept looking behind me. It felt like someone was staring at me but no one was there. Marco, stood next to me, when I spoke on my grandmother at the podium. A few others, stood up to speak and a woman from the church sung, I won't complain and she did an excellent job. I haven't been to church in a very long time but I did miss the singing.

At the burial, Shanta and my father, acted like a damn fool. She tried to get in the coffin with her and he laid on top of it. What the he'll were they thinking. My grandfather took his belt off and hit both of them on the legs. It made me laugh and Lord knows, I needed a good one. They were running around trying to get away from him, like kids. At one point, I thought, I would pee on myself, from laughing so hard. I shook my head and Marco, whispered in my ear, how weird my family was. Besides that, the service was beautiful, especially; when they let the doves fly at the end.

On the way to the repass, Marco rubbed my shoulders in the limo. My grandfather had his eyes closed and my cousin was talking to him, while me and his girl, chit chatted. Shanta, however; kept a snarl on her face and something about the way she stared, made me uncomfortable. I thought about asking but it would most likely, end up in an argument, so I let it go. We got out at the repast and I noticed Marco and Shanta, still standing at the limo, arguing.

"You ain't shit and the minute my niece finds out, I hope she leaves you for good." I heard Shanta say.

"What would be your reason for trying to hurt her with bullshit, that happened a long time ago?"

"Fuck her. If Cara, can't be happy, neither will she."

"Fuck me!"

"Yea, fuck you and him." His face became tight and I hugged him to relax. He's been doing his best, not killing her. I know, I should let him but she's still my aunt and I don't want her dead.

"What's going on and why would I leave him?" Shanta went to open her mouth and somebody called her name.

"Yea Marco. Tell her, before I do." She stormed off.

"You know, I love you right?" He made me face him.

"Yes. I love you too. What's wrong?"

"Ma, this isn't the right time to tell you."

"Tell me what?"

"Your aunt wants me to disclose some information to you. Unfortunately, it's not good."

"Just tell me. It can't be any worse than hearing, her daughter's trying to kill me."

"It's not but I promise to tell you tonight when we get home. I don't want her holding shit over me." He kissed my nose.

"Ok. Come eat." I grabbed his hand.

"Eat what?"

"Me later. But for now, food. You know we can go all night. At least, it will be on a full stomach." He licked his lips and smacked me on the ass.

"My girl gets freakier by the day."

"My man loves it."

"Yes, he does." We stepped in the repast together. People were speaking to me and he refused to let my hand go. He only did it, if I gave someone a hug.

We finally saw Ang and Tech, at a table and joined them. I got up and made both of us a plate and sat down. My grandfather, Rahmel, his girl Missy and a few other people, were sitting at the table with me, and my hateful aunt, sat at one across from us. Marco needs to tell me whatever she knows because I don't like the way she's staring at him.

"Baby, I'll be back." I stood up and so did he.

"I'm only going to the bathroom. Its right there." I saw him glancing around the room. Who was he looking for?

"I'm coming with you." He was adamant about me not leaving his sight.

"Silly, I don't need you to use the bathroom." I could tell he was struggling to let me go alone.

"Aight. I'm right here if you need me."

I kissed his cheek and made my way towards it. More people stopped me along the way and I turned around to see him smiling. Let me hurry, up so I can take my man home and do nasty things to him.

I opened the door and there were only two stalls and one was out of order. I went in to relieve myself, only to come out and see my worst nightmare standing in front of me. Actually, two of them were there, with stupid grins on their faces.

Cara

As I stood over my grandmothers' casket, letting the tears fall, all I could think of, is how I let her down. All she wanted, was for me to make up with Rakia and apologize to her. Unfortunately, her man isn't gonna allow me to live, whether I apologize or not. He already had people looking for me and I know that because his father, told my mom. It wasn't that I hated Rakia, I just hated the fact she got the man of my dreams. Why couldn't he love me the way her loved her? Why didn't he take the time out to get to know me? What was it about me, that is any different from her, besides being smart. I was gorgeous, had a nice body and would've done anything for him, had he given me a chance. But all of it, is out the window and now that my grandmother is gone, I'm gonna finish off what I started with Rakia. The bitch is going to find out Marco's little secret, he doesn't want her to know.

Yea, my mom told me they were over at the repast. She also mentioned, how she tried to tell Rakia before the funeral and again, right before they went into the repast. However, he blocked her from doing it both times. See, I learned a few things about Marco, from Bobbi and Mia. One… he loved sex. Two… Mia, was his first true love and coming back didn't work out the way she planned. And three… he would do anything for my cousin; including kill.

I admit, my ass cried a little, when I found out she was pregnant. My grandmother was ecstatic to be having two great grandchildren. We found out, not too long ago about Rahmel's chick expecting. It's too bad, she passed first. She would've been mad for me telling Marco's secret but who cares? She's been upset with me all this time; another few months wouldn't have hurt from her not speaking. I'm sure she's turning in her grave already knowing what I'm about to do.

On the drive over to the repast, Bobbi and I, smoked two blunts. At least, if I died, I'd be high. We stayed in the car until my mother came out. She told us where Rakia was sitting and how Marco wasn't allowing her outta his sight. The only way to get close to her, would be in the bathroom. She told us, she'd let us know, when she went in there. Being pregnant, meant using it a lot.

About ten minutes later, we got the text and both of us ran in through the back. My mom opened the door and we slid straight to the bathroom. You could see how crowded it was and I saw Tech and Marco, talking. My mom stood outside the door to tell people, it was broken and she was waiting on someone to unclog the toilet. The moment Rakia stepped out the stall, I could see fear and sadness on her face. *Boy, was this gonna be fun.*

"Hey cousin. Long time, no see." She looked past me, at Bobbi.

"Hi Cara, I didn't see you at the funeral. Did you like the service?" She grabbed a paper towel after washing her hands.

"It was nice. Anyway, I see your neck and arm healed up." I tried to touch it and she backed up.

"What do you want Cara?" I smirked and turned to look at Bobbi, who was doing the same.

"We wanna know." I pointed back and forth between, me and Bobbi.

"We wanna know, why you stole our man?"

"Cara, I didn't steal him from you and you know it. As far as this other woman, I didn't even know about her until the street party and he said, he wasn't with her."

"And you believed him?"

"Why wouldn't I?" She tried to move past, so I blocked her. I heard a tap on the door. My mom was telling me, either I was taking too long, or he was coming.

"Just like the gullible chick you are. He was still messing with both of us." She shook her head laughing.

"He stopped messing with Bobbi and we all know it, because he called her out in front of me." I looked at Bobbi, who shrugged her shoulders. The dumb bitch didn't even tell me.

"I know about the two of you, in New York. All you did was give him head and he didn't like it. He left and you tried again so he let you and then, on the way to Jersey. He blocked you and you've been stalking him ever since." I was shocked he gave her that little information but I was about to fuck her entire world up.

"Cara, I need to get back. If it's something you want, just say it." She sounded aggravated.

"I want you to make him see, I'm the woman for him." She scoffed up a laugh.

"Cara, I can't make him see anything."

"Sure, you can. Tell him, you have a disease that won't go away and then, send him my way."

"You sound crazy. Cara, he and I, have been intimate many times and he knows, my body is clean. I'm pregnant for God's sake." I sucked my teeth. He did tell me, she's the only woman, who he'd run up in raw.

"Well, figure it out."

"You're crazy." She shook her head in disappointment.

"If you didn't throw yourself at him, he'd be with me."

"You and I, both know that's not true."

"Did he ever tell you we fucked?" She stopped walking to the door and stared at me. I could tell, she was trying to figure out if I was lying.

"Yea, right. He wouldn't do that to me, regardless; if we were speaking or not." Now, it was my turn to laugh. I pulled my phone out, found what I was looking for and pressed play.

"Yes, Marco. Fuck, you feel so good."

"Shut the fuck up. You've wanted this dick, so take it." You heard him say. She covered her mouth.

Of course, Bobbi and I, set it up to record him. When I got to his house that night, we set the phone up and hit record, before he jumped out the shower. We knew she wouldn't believe he fucked me, because he always made it seem like he hated me. He may have caught me with the condom thing but he missed the camera. Granted, you couldn't really see much because it was dim in the room, but you damn sure heard us.

"Why Cara? How could you do that to me?"

"You're not woman enough for him."

"Why do you want him so bad?"

"He needs me and we both know it." She shook her head and let the tears fall.

"You can't be that delusional."

"You have no idea, bitch." I punched her in the face and she stumbled against the wall and fell.

"Oh my God, Cara." Bobbi yelled out. She was about to help her up but I snatched her away.

"OH NO!" Rakia yelled and I heard how scared she was.

"My water broke. Please get someone in here to help me." I smirked because it was too early for her to deliver.

"I think the bastard baby, needs to die. What you think Bobbi?"

"Cara, this isn't right. We need to get her help."

"If you even think about running your mouth, once we step out this bathroom. Its gonna be a problem." Yea, she was scared to death of me.

"But.-"

"But nothing."

"Cara, please. I'm bleeding and its hurting." She was hysterical crying. I snatched Bobbi's hand and walked out the door. I wish the fuck, I would help her.

"You were in there five minutes too long. Did you tell her?" My mom asked.

"Yup, and she's upset." Is all I said and made my way through the crowd of people.

I made sure not to look at Marco but it was impossible, when I wanted to see my future man. The way I see it, is after my cousin bleeds to death, he'll mourn and I'll be right there to help him through it. Unfortunately, once our eyes met, I knew it would be a problem. He stood up and glanced around the hall. I'm assuming he was looking for Rakia. Tech, must've noticed something too because he was right behind him. Outta nowhere, Rahmel, Ang and my grandfather stood up and their eyes landed on me.

I shrugged my shoulders and went to give my great aunt a hug. Not too long after, I felt an excruciating pain in my arm. I turned around and Marco was coming towards me full speed, with his gun pointed at me. People were screaming and running but he was focused, solely on me. *Why didn't I just leave?*

To Be Continued...

CPSIA information can be obtained
at www.ICGtesting.com
Printed in the USA
LVHW011658180119
604419LV00014B/578/P